P9-AOL-499

Dead End

The agent set the book down. The room had a ghostly air and gave him the impression of a town that no longer existed because it lay under water. "No television," he said. "Not even a radio."

"No, Not even a wallet. No bankbook, no checkbook, only that money the detective came up with in the bottom bureau drawer. Three hundred dollars. Six fifties in an envelope."

"Where the hell would she have gotten that? Especially fifties."

"Mad money?"

"A hell of a lot of mad money, but it could be..."

"Fingerprints?"

"Every readable print in the room is hers."

The other agent sighed hard. "Beautiful." He removed his glasses to polish them. His naked eyes were small and bitter. "She created herself," he said softly. "She told lies within lies, and tomorrow we bury her under a name that probably wasn't hers."

The stout agent said nothing. The room was close, and sweat tickled his face.

The other agent, glasses in hand, said, "So who the Christ was she?"

the baby-sitter

Andrew Coburn

PUBLISHED BY POCKET BOOKS NEW YORK

POCKET BOOKS, a Simon & Schuster division of
GULF & WESTERN CORPORATION
1230 Avenue of the Americas, New York, N.Y. 10020

Copyright © 1979 by Andrew Coburn

Published by arrangement with W. W. Norton & Co., Inc.
Library of Congress Catalog Card Number: 78-24150

All rights reserved, including the right to reproduce
this book or portions thereof in any form whatsoever.
For information address W. W. Norton & Co., Inc.,
500 Fifth Avenue, New York, N.Y. 10036

ISBN: 0-671-82864-9

First Pocket Books printing May, 1980

10 9 8 7 6 5 4 3 2 1

POCKET and colophon are trademarks of Simon & Schuster.

Printed in the U.S.A.

Acknowledgments

Nikki Smith, Peter Skolnik, Starling Lawrence, Jean DeRosa, and Norma Nathan for help past and present.

For my wife,
Bernadine Casey Coburn,
and our friends the Meades.

the baby-sitter

1

"My wife," John Wright said with a start, realizing he had lost track of her.

"She's all right."

She was not all right, and neither was he. His hair was saturated with sweat, though the kitchen was cool, and he could not remember whether Merle had gone to the bedroom or the bathroom. They had had words over whether she should stay on her feet. That was hours ago, and it was past daybreak now, the sun streaking the windows, birds making a racket.

"Sit down, Mr. Wright."

Two men at the table were questioning him, asking things put to him earlier by others, his answers unsatisfactory now, sometimes out of sinc, for he was only half hearing the questions.

"Do you mind?" he said but did not wait for an answer. Standing at the sink, he took a healthy shot of bourbon and let it burn. His grip on the glass was fierce. The window over the sink was open, and his ear was tuned to the birds, as if listening to them would make everything normal again. His eye picked up the fire of phlox, planted by his wife, miraculously untrampled, despite the many men roaming the back lawn in search of something.

"Mr. Wright."

He turned, his face frozen. "I don't understand. I'm nobody. I'm not rich or famous or influential. I'm only a teacher. I don't even have tenure."

"Sit down, Mr. Wright."

The voice was like a recording, and Wright took a stricken step, empty glass in hand, as if expecting somebody to refill it. "I don't know any gangsters or crazies, no one who'd do this."

"Please, Mr. Wright."

A hand gestured, and he slumped into a chair, aware of the movement of other men throughout the house. He couldn't keep them straight and had no idea who was in charge or whether anybody was. The two sitting across from him looked like businessmen. One wore silver-rimmed glasses and was lean and stiff, and the other appeared soft.

"I'm trying to keep up with you people," Wright said. "Are you fellows also from the district attorney's office?"

"Federal Bureau of Investigation," said the one with the glasses. "If you don't mind, Mr. Wright, we'd like to backtrack a bit. Last night you and your wife went to a movie."

"Yes, a movie," Wright said automatically. A movie in Boston, a mediocre one, and then a bite at Brigham's, and then they had driven through dark tepid heat on Route 93, four lanes of fast traffic, hot taillights, and an occasional daredevil driver. He had kept to the inside lane at a reasonable speed, his arm around Merle, their intimacy still special after ten years of marriage.

"And you got home about eleven-forty."

"Yes, home." Home was Exit 15, Ballardville, a town of twelve thousand, a bedroom of Boston. Home was a seven-room garrison protected by shrubs and trees, with a rear guard of willows near the leeching field. Home was where they had expected at least one light burning, if not in their daughter's room, then certainly in the den, where the babysitter spread her books. The house was black.

"You mentioned suspecting something was wrong."

"The front door was ajar," Wright said, remembering Merle at his shoulder, the two of them edging together. "I pushed it open."

Pushed it open, groped for the switch, lit the front hall, and saw blood on his fingers, some on the wall and more on the floor. He had tried to block Merle, force her back, but she was nailed in place and screaming near his ear. The sitter lay in the light, her head no longer whole.

"You tracked blood."

"We couldn't help it."

"Did you notice any other footprints?"

"We saw only Paula." Her blouse ripped open and her breasts bare but unmarked, as if the killer had merely been curious. Her jeans were secure.

Wright rose with the empty shot glass, and the agent with the glasses misinterpreted the move. "We'd rather you wouldn't, Mr. Wright. Have coffee instead."

"Where's my wife?"

"She's fine, Mr. Wright. Don't worry."

Both agents waited patiently for him to sit down again. They kept their eyes fixed on him in the manner of scientists awaiting a chemical reaction, perhaps explosive.

He remained on his feet, remembering the way Merle had stumbled past the body and started for the stairs, her voice deep enough to have come out of a drum: *My baby!*

"What should I tell her?"

The other agent, as if silently commanded to speak, said, "Sir. It'd be easier if you sat down."

"Can I say you'll find her?"

The agent with the glasses sat back, letting the other one take over. "Sit down, sir."

"Is my daughter alive?"

"We're working on that assumption, sir. We have no evidence to the contrary. Sir, sit—"

"Please don't tell me that again. And don't lie to me. I couldn't take it."

The agent with the glasses straightened. "No one's lying to you, Mr. Wright. No one intends to. And you can stand or sit, but please answer our questions."

Wright sat down, squeezing the shot glass. He seemed dazed.

"That's better," the agent with the glasses said. "Let's get back to the victim. Her last name was Aherne."

Wright nodded.

"And she was a student at the community college, where you teach?"

Wright rubbed his forehead and slid his fingers into his hair. "I've been through all of these questions."

"Not with us you haven't."

Wright shoved the shot glass to one side and rose awkwardly. "I'll be back."

"Where are you going?"

"My wife."

The agents watched him leave, the one with glasses drumming his fingers on the table. The other one said, "Do you want me to bring him back?"

"No. I want you to see the coroner before anybody else does."

2

"Weapon was a hammer, I'm sure of it," said the assistant medical examiner, a short man in a suit that was buff-colored, like a file folder. He had a smooth well-fed face, high forehead and button eyes.

"No hammers in the house," said the agent. "Except one for tacks."

"I repeat, weapon was a hammer, one with heft."

"Sorry. Go on."

The doctor referred to his notes with a sigh, as if he were much put upon. "Everything is always rush-rush with you federal fellows, isn't it? We've only done a partial autopsy, you understand."

The agent nodded.

"All right. This is preliminary, what I'm telling you. The skull was fractured and the brain damage massive. Picture somebody with a strong arm doing it, someone at least two inches taller than the victim. Nothing remarkable about her body, no surgical scars. Five-foot-six, hundred-ten pounds. Kept herself nice and clean. Her teeth were OK because she was young, but they weren't that well taken care of. Probably hadn't been to a dentist in years."

"How old do you think she was?"

"Eighteen or nineteen."

"Was she pregnant?"

"No."

"Was she a virgin?"

"No."

"Was she molested?"

"No evidence she was, and no traces of semen." The doctor smiled. "She did, however, have a little talcum powder down there. I knew a nurse years ago did that. Had everything I could do to keep from sneezing into her system."

The agent did not react to the doctor's laugh. He asked, "Was she on drugs?"

"No evidence of that," the doctor said, sobering.

"Could she have touched her killer?"

"Nothing in the nails, no foreign hairs."

"Have you fixed the time?"

"Between nine and ten, closer to nine."

The agent referred to his own notes as the doctor put his away. The doctor stood motionless, smiling professionally.

"Any theories of your own?"

"I'd say she was struck without a word of warning but saw it coming. Then, she was struck repeatedly by somebody in a rage."

"Just in the head?"

"Right. And when she was down."

"And you're sure about the time?"

"Yes," the doctor said with a faint show of impatience. "When the autopsy's completed and the results are all in, you'll get everything in writing."

"We appreciate this early information."

The doctor smiled. "Remember me at Christmastime."

Ballardville Police Chief Edmund Tull, wearing a poplin jacket over his white uniform shirt, stopped Wright and led him to one side. "You can't use the stairs yet, Mr. Wright. Everything's still blocked off."

"My wife."

"She's OK, honest. Your doctor's been and gone. I think she's sleeping."

Wright plowed a hand through his hair as Chief Tull gazed at him sadly. The chief was tall and balding and had a moist burning face, with splotches, like a diaper rash.

"I want to help you, Mr. Wright. Jesus, I want to help you. But those Feds aren't going to tell me anything; I can see that. They like to keep things to themselves and run the whole show. I know that, though they act like it's not so."

"Who did this, Chief?"

"I've got theories, and I'm already checking them out. I know things in this town no one else does."

"Find my daughter."

"Mr. Wright, I'll do everything I can." He placed a raw hand on Wright's shoulder. "Neighbors want to know what they can do for you. The woman next door wants to send over a meal."

"No, nothing." Wright came alive. "What about the neighbors?"

"They didn't see or hear anything, Mr. Wright."

"Maybe they're lying. They might be afraid."

"They're afraid, Mr. Wright, but I don't think they're lying."

Again Wright swept a hand through his hair, which was fine, light brown, seldom in place. He was as tall as the chief but at least twenty-five pounds lighter. His face was drained.

The chief parted his poplin jacket and exposed a small revolver sticking out of the waistband of his police pants. He patted the butt of it. "I've got something bigger than this at home. I'll catch the sonofabitch did this, I'll kill him. That's between you and me, Mr. Wright."

Wright faltered and with a cracked voice said, "It's my daughter I'm—"

"Yes, I know, Mr. Wright. I know what's going on in your head, but we'll find her. You've got my personal guarantee."

Wright took a breath. "I'm going outside for some air. Just for a minute."

The chief stopped him. "Don't want to do that, Mr. Wright. Reporters from Boston are out there, even a TV crew. You don't want to see those people."

Wright felt helpless, as if he were a child impersonating an adult. He pointed to the stairs. "My wife's up there. I've got to see her."

The chief let him go, and Wright pushed hard past a rope, stepping on plastic sheeting where the body had been. More sheeting hung from the wall and fluttered ghostlike as he passed.

Merle was not asleep. She stared down at him from the top of the stairs, fully dressed, her shoes in her hands, as if someone had taken them and returned them. She stood on slender legs that appeared ready to give. A neighbor, Mrs. Harrington next door, had once described her as comely. She was, in fact, beautiful, reminiscent of Gene Tierney in her prime. Gene Tierney about to tumble down the stairs.

Wright took the stairs three at a time.

The district attorney, flanked by the burly state detective assigned to his office, stood on the sidewalk outside the Wrights' house and read a statement before cameras: "My office in conjunction with federal, state and local authorities is investigating a homicide and an apparent kidnaping at the home of Mr. and Mrs. John Wright. The homicide victim was babysitting at the time, and her identity is being withheld pending notification of next of kin. The apparent kidnap victim is Marcie Wright, aged fourteen months. No ransom demands have been made up to this time. The concerted investigation is intense, and further statements will be issued by this office in due course."

"How was the victim killed?" a print reporter yelled out.

"She was bludgeoned," the DA said and turned, allowing no more questions. Uniformed state police immediately created a barrier. The DA and the detective lumbered past sawhorses scattered about to keep the unauthorized at bay. A young assistant DA, who looked young enough to have just passed the bar, waited under a red maple that dominated the front lawn. When he figured he'd waited long enough, he stepped briskly forward.

"Something funny with the Feds, sir. They've been huddling. I think they know something."

The DA calmly regarded his assistant, who wore a large class ring from Boston University School of Law. The DA had graduated from Suffolk Law, second-rate in comparison. The DA said, "What do they know?"

"I'll try to find out."

"Do that, kid."

"Something else, sir. The crank calls have started. Some are downright sadistic. Feds let me listen to one."

"There'll be a lot of that stuff," the DA said with a faint wheeze. "It's just beginning. OK, get back to the Feds. I want your nose right up their asses."

The young man backed off. The DA whipped out a handkerchief and swabbed his broad face marked by burst capillaries in his cheeks. "What do you think?" he asked the detective, who coughed. His name was Harty, and he was near retirement.

"It's not your usual snatch," he said.

"Don't tell me something I already know. If a legitimate ransom call comes in, I'll be damned surprised. The kook calls, that's all we'll get."

"This could be a double homicide," the detective said. "That's what I thought from the first. The kid could be lying under a bush somewhere, could've been dumped down a sewer or heaved in the woods. No problem disposing of a body that small."

"This case could get national coverage, you know that?" The DA stuffed away his handkerchief. "Go on, I'm listening."

"Could've been a burglar," the detective said. "Weirdo type, maybe an addict. Panics when he sees the sitter and clobbers her, then grabs the baby on impulse."

"Did you hear what the weapon was? A hammer. What kind of burglar goes around with a hammer?"

"It's got a claw on it. Why not? On the other hand, it could've been a peeping Tom, a pervert who went berserk in the balls. I told the chief to give me a list of his loonies."

"She wasn't raped."

"Maybe his zipper didn't work. Or maybe it was the baby he wanted." The detective brushed his shirt pocket for cigarettes that weren't there. He was trying to quit. "Or it could've been someone the sitter knew, a boy friend. At the moment I'm leaning that way. I'll feel a hell of a lot better when we know more about her."

"What about Mrs. Wright? Nobody's even talked to her yet."

The detective shrugged. "It's like she's in a coma. A vegetable."

The DA traced a slow finger under his mouth. "A goodlooking woman. How old did you say she is?"

"Thirty-six."

"Christ, she doesn't look it. They only had that one kid, huh?"

The detective nodded. "That's a funny situation. In a town like this women her age either go back to school or into real estate. Her situation was reversed. She gave up a good job and had a kid."

"And they haven't been in the town that long. What, two years? What made them come here? What kind of people are they? Maybe they take LSD or something. Check on them."

"Feds are already doing it. So far they seem OK. They came here, I guess, because they wanted to get out of the rat race. They both worked for an advertising agency, same one."

Again the DA slid a finger under his mouth. Then he said, "Watch the news tonight. Let me know how I sounded."

Wright sat by the bed like a visitor and watched his wife break momentarily out of sleep. "What day is it?" she asked, as if she thought several had passed.

Then her eyes closed. A little later someone rapped lightly on the door, and Wright rose stiffly.

The agent spoke from the partly open door: "How is she, Mr. Wright?"

"Medicated. She's under, but I don't know for how long."

"How are you doing?"

"I'm all right."

"Could you come downstairs?"

"I'd rather stay with her."

"It's important we talk again."

The agent led the way down, over the plastic, and gestured toward the living room, as if the house were his now, federal property. Wright hesitated.

"I'd rather step outside. I really need the air."

They went just beyond the front steps and stood on the grass. It was dusk, and tiny black flies hovered near their faces, the flies in a seemingly immobile cluster, like a mass of tacks hammered into the air. Wright's car, a four-year-old Cutlass, was parked as he and Merle had left it, but he had a chill from the inexplicable impression that somebody had been in it and through it.

"Tell me more about Paula Aherne," the agent said, relaxing his stance. His silver-rimmed glasses appeared glued to his face.

"She was quiet," Wright said, "and very caring about my daughter. She adored Marcie. They adored each other."

"By quiet, do you mean secretive?"

"No," Wright said, staring at the agent through the network of flies. "I never once thought of her that way. She was reserved and certainly a little shy."

"Did you have her in any of your classes?"

"We've been through this."

The agent swiped the air. "I know, Mr. Wright, but it's necessary to go over things. Give it to me again, please, how she started sitting for you."

"I put a notice on the bulletin board. That was back in January, right after the start of the semester. She sat for us once a week, Fridays, our evening out, and she often dropped in on my wife in the late afternoon to visit and to see Marcie. That was the highlight of Marcie's day, and my wife enjoyed having her there."

"She did?"

"Yes."

"You and your wife took to her right away."

"Yes."

The agent raised a hand and quietly cleared his throat. "She wasn't wearing a bra. I suppose that's the way girls are today, not like in my time and probably not in yours. Must be a lot of that at the college."

Wright merely stared.

The agent smiled. "Of course Paula Aherne wasn't really that big, so I suppose it didn't matter all that much."

"What are you asking me?"

"Take it easy, Mr. Wright. I'm only trying to get a line on her. Are you certain she never had anyone over when she sat for you? A boy friend?"

"I'm sure. We had a rule about that, and I know she wouldn't have broken it."

"How do you know that?"

"I just know."

"She was quite attractive."

"Yes."

Neighbors passed by in a car, and Wright felt their eyes. He was even more conscious of the agent's eyes. They had turned grave.

"Did you have anything going with her, Mr. Wright?"

"Jesus Christ," he said in a voice barely audible, as if he feared raising it because the agent might be seeking a pathological twist in him. He remembered with panic an innocent touch, his hand on her hip as he had helped her into his car to drive her home. She had had books in her arms. He remembered another time, his eyes caught in the pale flash of flesh between her shirt and jeans as she had scooped up Marcie. He remembered the sunniness of her hair, which was short and curly and drew light.

"I'm sorry," the agent said. "It was something I had to ask."

"I understand," Wright murmured, his body rigid. The agent moved closer, through the flies.

"Think about this for a moment, Mr. Wright. All you actually know about her is what she told you, isn't that so?"

Wright felt that he was being hit with too much too fast, with no chance to sort things out. The sky was rapidly darkening, blotting out parts of the yard. He stared at the agent with a vague fear.

The agent said, "She told you her parents were dead."

"Yes. They were killed on the Southeast Expressway when she was five."

"That was convenient," the agent said softly.

"What?"

"That's what she told you? They were killed on the expressway."

"That's what she told my wife. Weren't they?"

"We don't know. She also told you she was born in Boston and mentioned an aunt. An aunt you never met."

"There was no reason for me to meet her aunt. But her aunt's alive. She lives in Boston."

The agent shook his head. "We can't locate her."

"The Dorchester section."

"Yes, we know. We still can't locate her."

Wright did not speak. His face was numb. He watched the agent bat the flies.

"So far, Mr. Wright, nothing you've told us about her is checking out. She wasn't even enrolled at the college. She was merely monitoring classes, on her own, apparently without permission. Were you aware of that?"

Wright did not respond.

"What I'm saying, Mr. Wright, is we don't know who the hell she was. We don't even know for sure Paula Aherne was her name."

Wright saw a slice of the moon.

"Did you hear me, Mr. Wright?"

Wright heard him, but he could think of nothing to say.

3

She appeared at the doorway of his cubbyhole office, her face moist from hurrying. She held a jacket and a book in her arms and was wearing an oversized wool sweater, jeans, and Adidas sneakers. She made a slight noise to gain his attention.

She had seen the notice on the board and was interested.

"Come in and sit down," he said, a bit apologetically, for the chair near his desk was crooked, and she needed to sit carefully. She folded her jacket across her lap and rested her hands on her book. He, sitting back, questioned her casually. She had a faintly shy way of answering, of looking at him, which he found refreshing. Recently another young woman sitting in that crooked chair, practically falling out of it on purpose, had flirted with him for a good grade and had given him a kiss-my-ass look when she hadn't gotten it. This one seemed taciturn as if by nature, and he offered her a cigarette to put her at ease.

She didn't smoke. Her book, a New Directions paperback, nearly slipped from her lap. A John Hawkes novel.

"What class is that?"

"No, I'm reading this on my own."

She wasn't trying to impress him, he could see that. She was embarrassed she had said it. He said, "Do you like Hawkes?"

"Yes, I think so."

He smiled. "His heroes are usually pretty gloomy, victims of cruel jokes, the cruelest being their own lives."

"I also like Faulkner," she said, as if determined to overcome her awkwardness.

"I do too. But another gloomy fellow."

"I like his women," she said, tipping a little in the chair. "They know how to survive."

"Faulkner's word was *prevail*."

"He's dead?"

"Yes."

"I didn't know that, but I thought he might be."

Wright liked what he saw. He liked the short cut of her hair, which looked freshly washed, and he liked the intensity of her gray-green eyes, which never seemed to blink. He continued his questions, and she told him that this was her first semester at the college and that she wasn't on a full schedule but was easing her way in after less-than-adequate high school years in Boston.

"I suppose the busing situation didn't help."

She shook her head.

"You were born in Boston?"

"Yes, but I'm glad to be out of it for a while. That's why I came here."

He asked about her parents.

"They're dead. They died when I was little, and I lived with my aunt in Dorchester."

He knew Dorchester relatively well and said, "What street?" She told him, but he couldn't place it.

"My aunt works at Sears," she offered. "She's a

senior sales clerk, practically in charge of a department. She's been there for years. She pays for my room here in town."

"Where's that?"

"Parker Street," she said and told him the name and number of the rooming house. He knew exactly where it was, off the center of town, a half-hour walk to the college and slightly more than that, in the opposite direction, to his house.

"Do you like Ballardville?" he asked, watching her readjust her jacket while keeping a firm hold on her book. She jerked forward.

"Very much."

"My wife and I like it too, though we're not that much a part of it yet; busy, I guess. We've been here two years. We're from Boston too."

She tipped to one side.

"Sorry about that chair."

They exchanged a smile, and he brought the subject back to her schedule, her classes. She mentioned her Introductory Psych instructor and said, "I don't think he knows my name yet. It's such a big class."

"Yes, a few of mine are. I teach English and some literature courses."

"Yes, I know," she said.

He sat forward with a glance at his watch. "By the way, it would only be one night a week. Fridays. That's usually the only time my wife and I go out."

"Fridays are fine," she said at once, "and any other time. I love children."

He told her about his daughter and was struck by the way she listened with an eagerness too intense to doubt. His words seemed to absorb her, as if anything said about a child were precious.

"We just have the one," he said and then, as if needing to explain, added, "We waited."

She seemed pleased that he should tell her that, as if entrusting her with a family secret, and she said, "I was an only child."

He smiled. "Then you may find yourself coming into a houseful of them. I was an only child, so was my wife, and Marcie probably will be. At least that's the idea."

He jotted down his address and telephone number and arranged for her to meet Merle.

"I like her," Merle said. "She's a child herself."

"You saw that."

"Yes. A child, but I think a very responsible one."

They were sitting on the rug near the fire watching the eleven o'clock news on a small Sony Wright had toted in from the kitchen. She was perched on a pillow and was wearing a flannel nightgown gathered up in her lap. He had a small bourbon on the rocks, and she was sipping Sabra.

He asked, "How'd she get along with Marcie?"

"Marvelous. You had to be there."

The fire was jagged, overly bright, flames bursting out of a crumbling log, ashes fierce with orange embers. The news was about gunfire in the Mideast, Cubans in Africa, a street murder in Roxbury, *Saturday Night Fever* at the movies.

Wright said, "I think this is her first babysitting job."

"It is, but she's a natural."

"I knew you'd like her."

They turned their eyes to the fire during a string of commercials and then listened to the weather forecast: sunless and cold tomorrow and a fifty percent chance of snow the following day. Wright rattled the ice in his glass and yawned. He had spent a good part of the evening grading student essays. Merle smiled, holding him with her charcoal eyes, which always warmed him, the eyes set firmly over high white cheekbones.

"What's the matter?" he asked.

"Wondering about you. Be truthful, do you ever miss the old apartment?"

"Does that include the triple locks on the door?"

"I'm serious."

"Sure I miss it, at times, but never enough to want to go back."

"You don't miss Boston?"

He stretched his stockinged feet closer to the fire. "I like it when we go in. I like the theaters and the restaurants, but I wouldn't want to live there again."

"Honestly?"

"Hey." He shifted closer to her and touched her cheek, heated from the fire and the Sabra. "Why the questions?"

She shrugged.

"I get it," he said with a laugh. "You heard me cursing over those papers. I always do that—and some of those essays weren't that bad, that's a fact."

"I feel responsible," she said, her gaze level. "Practically everything we've done in the last few years has been my idea."

"But then it became as much mine, even more in some cases, especially about having Marcie. So don't take all the glory."

"What about changing jobs?"

"Come on, Merle. Could you picture either of us writing copy the rest of our lives?"

"You could have gone higher."

"How the hell high could I have taken an ulcer? I'd have gotten one." He finished off his bourbon. "And as I recall, you were the one got a kick out of chasing accounts."

"Only for a while," she said. "Here, want a sip of this?"

"You haven't much left."

"I said a sip. Take a little one."

He did. And they held hands as the sports announcer spoke disparagingly of the faltering Celtics and passionately of the winning Bruins, teams she was totally familiar with, for he had often taken her to the Garden. He was twenty-eight and she two years younger when they met at the ad agency, she new to the job, he a relatively old hand and on the rise. It was attraction at first sight. They had not been in a hurry to marry; yet within three months, perfectly sure of what they were doing, they drove to Kennebunk, Maine, and held hands before a justice of the peace who, winking at his wife, a witness, gave them a choice of a short or a long service. They spent two weeks at a beachside hotel, acquiring no tan, only a pink blush that they wore back to the agency.

The news ended with jokes by the anchormen, followed fast by more commercials. Merle lifted her glass and drained it. The fire colored her face and throat and made her look vaguely Oriental. Johnny Carson was coming on.

"Who's going to switch it?" he asked.

"What else is on?"

She rubbed an eye. "There might be a movie on seven."

"Want to watch it?"

"No, but see what it is."

He swung far to one side and changed channels. She dipped back to retrieve cigarettes and matches, her pale legs angling out and her gown rising. The fire exposed her, painting hidden flesh, and Wright glimpsed the dark surge of hair at the cleft. He reached for her.

"This is why I wouldn't want to go back to the apartment. We didn't have a fireplace."

"Bed would be better," she said.

"And you're not the romantic you were."

"Says who?"

The flames painted them both, and the hard orange heat soon drove them to a cooler spot on the rug.

A persistently cold springtime, but always a warm welcome for Paula, a pop-in visitor, whether she was sitting that evening or not. She and Merle took Marcie outdoors, where tulip sprouts were shivering out of the wet ground. Paula gathered the child up in her arms and pointed to a naked oak branch, to the ancient lizard-look of a bird whose eye was beaded in on them. The child was affectionate, and strands of her dark hair snagged her sudden offering of a kiss, the kiss like a pinprick. Paula stared into the sumptuous eyes, and Merle, standing to one side, laughed.

"You've really found a friend there."

"She's beautiful."

Merle smiled, almost defensively. "Sometimes I can't believe she's mine. That I produced her."

"You're lucky."

"Yes, I think I am."

Paula hugged the child harder. "I can't believe *I* was ever that little. Maybe I wasn't."

Sunlight webbed the golden branches of willows. The child wanted down, and Paula complied. The women talked, Merle in a bulky cardigan belonging to her husband, Paula in her familiar jacket and jeans. They wandered near a strangled drift of barely budding hedge-rose, which had kept a couple of mockingbirds in berries during the winter. A broken bell of birdseed hung nearby.

Merle said, "I can't wait to start gardening. I didn't do too well last year, except with the flowers."

"I'll help you," Paula said. "I'd like to learn."

Merle smiled. "We should do great. Two city girls with big thumbs, not necessarily green."

"Look!"

Paula was pointing, talking to the child, not to Merle. A squirrel, the perfect aerialist, leaped from a willow to an oak. Marcie missed it. Paula ran to her, heaved her up, and pointed again. The squirrel was scaling branches, as if showing off.

Merle approached, her hands stuck deep in the cardigan.

"I love her," Paula said quietly, as if explaining, bouncing Marcie to a more comfortable position.

"And I wish I had a camera."

"I'd pay you to mind her."

"Your teddy bear, mine too," Merle said, as if they were sisters with a toy.

"I suppose when you have a child, you become one."

"Even before," Merle said, pulling out a handkerchief to wipe Marcie's nose. "When I was carrying her, I had fantasies wolves were in the yard, prowling the dark. You start believing in the more violent fairy tales again."

"I like fairy tales," Paula said. "But not that kind. I like the ones you sing to babies."

Merle laughed. "When are you going to get married, Paula?"

"I like to think about babies but not about husbands," Paula said. She was solemn but only for a second.

Later, in the house, Paula on her knees and urging her on, Marcie used the potty, making extravagantly unnecessary noises, and rose from a tiny deposit of fudge.

Paula applauded, and Merle lifted her coffee cup in a half salute.

Merle scanned the newspaper and read aloud an item with a California dateline, a brisk account of an ailing middle-aged woman who had driven cross-country, a grueling journey, a death trip, for when the woman reached Sacramento, her birthplace, she did away with herself.

Merle shook her head. "A tragedy reduced to a half-dozen paragraphs."

Paula, with Marcie again in her arms, peered at the piece and said, "My parents got less than that."

Merle quietly closed the newspaper. "Do you miss them?" she asked.

"I've never stopped."

Merle wanted to hug her in the same way her own child was being hugged. Instead she reached for her coffee and said nothing, as if silence were in order. She felt Paula's eyes leave her. She knew exactly where they had gone—to Marcie.

As if the two of them had secrets.

4

Chief Tull stood deep in thought in front of the Wrights' house as one of his officers approached him. The officer was young and had gum in his mouth, a slow chewer, his jaws barely moving. "Anything breaking?" he asked nonchalantly.

The chief scarcely acknowledged him. He had liked him well enough when he hired him off the Civil Service list, but since then the young man had let his hair grow over his ears and over the back of his collar.

"We're still involved, aren't we, Chief? The Feds and the state guys aren't going to push us out, are they?"

"Nobody pushes us out."

"Any ransom call yet?"

The chief shook his head.

"This is the second day," the officer said. "Don't you think there should've been one by now?"

The chief shrugged.

"Tell you what I heard, Chief. There isn't going to be a ransom call. The kid's dead."

"Who told you that?"

"Couple of the troopers."

"What do they know!" the chief said in a tone of disgust. He had a son nearly the officer's age. The son smoked dope and didn't work. "There's a man and woman suffering in there," the chief said, pointing at the house, "and that's the last thing they want to hear, that their daughter's dead."

"What do you think?"

"I don't know."

"This is where cloning would come in handy, Chief. You know what cloning is, don't you?" The chief didn't, but he didn't say so. He toed the grass. The officer hooked his thumbs in the loops of his pants, and said, "That's what parents should do. Clone each kid, so if they lose one they've got a duplicate."

The chief caught the drift and clenched his fists. He wanted to wipe the grin off the officer's face. Again he pointed, this time in a different direction, and said in a dead-calm voice, "I want you to go back to the station. I want you to stay away from this house."

The officer started to speak and then changed his mind and rapidly backed off.

"She didn't have much," the agent with the silver glasses said. "Certainly not much of a wardrobe."

Two pairs of well-worn jeans, three shirts, some socks, a few blank T-shirts, a bra, several pairs of bikini underpants, one of them candy-striped. A winter jacket. A wool sweater. Red mittens.

"Plus what she had on," said the second agent, who was stout. He held up the bra. "At least we know she wore one once in a while." He reached for the candy-striped underpants. "What do you think of these?"

The agent with the glasses did not look. He was gazing about as if measuring the room, which was small, with nothing on the walls, not even a calendar. The room held a neatly made bed, a bureau, a table and chair for studying, an old floor lamp that seemed to have been used back and forth between table and bed. The bulb in the ceiling was weak. An empty Coca-Cola can was in the wastebasket.

"Poor little bitch," he said half under his breath.

Two towels. No face cloth. A bulging vinyl pouch containing toothbrush and Pepsodent, Dial soap, loose Tampax, throwaway razor, Prell shampoo. No cosmetics. No contraceptives. No pills of any kind, not even aspirin.

"No clock," the stout agent said. "And she wasn't wearing a watch. How the hell did she keep time?"

"With her feet," the agent with the glasses said, moving to the table, glancing at the text books, apparently bought second-hand at the college book store. Many paperbacks, some of them quality. A ball-point pen. A loose-leaf notebook, lecture notes on three subjects: history, psychology, sociology. No graded papers. No private ones. No diary, no pictures or letters, no souvenirs.

He picked up one of the quality paperbacks. Its cover depicted a naked black woman carrying a bundle on her head, the face of the sun gazing at her, a bird gliding toward her. "*Second Skin* by John Hawkes." He flipped pages. "Ever hear of it?"

The stout agent shrugged and said, "No jewelry, and she wasn't wearing any. No receipts except for rent, starting last January. That's when she started monitoring classes. Took a lot of her meals at the college cafeteria. Cheapest place for her. She certainly didn't eat here."

The other agent set the book down. The room had

a ghostly air and gave him the impression of a town that no longer existed because it lay under water. "No television," he said. "Not even a radio."

"Nothing. The state people went over this place pretty good."

"You were here when they did, I hope."

"You bet your life I was."

"No Social Security card?"

"No. Not even a wallet. No bank book, no check book, only that money the detective came up with in the bottom bureau drawer. Three-hundred dollars. Six fifties in an envelope."

"Where the hell would she have gotten that? Especially fifties."

"Mad money?"

"A hell of a lot of mad money, but it could be. Did she have visitors?"

"People here aren't sure, but they don't think so. She was quiet and polite and kept to herself. Toilet's down the hall. They say she always left it clean."

"Fingerprints?"

"Every readable print in the room is hers."

The other agent sighed hard. "Beautiful." He removed his glasses to polish them. His naked eyes were small and bitter. "She created herself," he said softly. "She told lies within lies, and tomorrow we bury her under a name that probably wasn't hers."

The stout agent said nothing. The room was close, and sweat tickled his face.

The other agent, glasses still in hand, said, "So who the Christ was she?"

Wright switched on the Sony in the kitchen and forced himself to watch the eleven o'clock news, his stomach shifting when a stark sketch of Paula Aherne filled the twelve-inch screen. The state police artist had produced a vague but eerie likeness, had even given her a smile, an uncomplicated one, which wasn't hers. Hers had been soft, guarded, fast to fade. Then, without warning, his daughter's picture appeared, a blow-up of the one he had extracted from a frame and surrendered to a federal agent. He could not bear to look.

The house was mostly dark. Men dozed in chairs in the living room, their tape recorder and other equipment resting near telephones. Outside a hatless state trooper sat slouched in a prowl car, perhaps asleep, though probably not. Wright peered through a window at an exceptionally bright moon that was burning the trees, the grass. The trooper was not asleep. He and Wright traded a glance through barriers of glass.

The barricading rope was gone from the hall, and the pale plastic sheeting had been removed from the wall but not from the floor. It crackled under Wright's shoes like fire. The wall had been washed—Chief Tull had seen to it—but traces of the stains remained. Wright stiffened. The house no longer seemed his.

He climbed the dark stairs quietly, not wanting to disturb the two agents in the living room, and paused at the top. Perhaps if he entered his daughter's room now he'd find her there. He imagined himself rousing Merle with Marcie in his arms.

But he could not play the game.

He entered his own bedroom with no show of lights. Merle was a ghostly sprawl in the moonlight, her hair floating over the pillow, the sheet snagged around her. He slipped past the bad and into the bathroom, flipping on the fluorescent light. His unshaved face flashed in the mirror and frightened him. He sprinkled aspirin into his hand and swallowed them dry, a trick he had mastered at the ad agency. Eyes closed, he tried to rub away a knot of tension in his neck.

"Let me do it," Merle said.

He whirled.

She stood in the doorway, viewing him as if through a special prism. Her smile was totally unmotivated and her lower lip loose as if she had no control over it. Then she was in his arms, weightless, the front of her gown bunched and damp.

"Hold me."

He was.

She lifted her chin and brought a hand to his face. "You look terrible."

He took her hand. The delicate blue veins, put there as if by a ballpoint, had become hot-red threads. He kissed the fingers and said, "I thought you were asleep."

"I was."

He could smell her medication. Her hair was full of sweat. She was purposely not asking him anything, as if anticipating unacceptable answers. He pushed the hair from her face.

"I called Arizona. I spoke with your father."

"Oh," she said, but she did not want to talk about that either, as if for the time being much had to be bottled up, saved for a safer day. "What time is it?" she asked.

He told her.

"Have you eaten?"

"Yes," he lied.

"I haven't done any food-shopping."

"There's plenty."

She sagged in his arms, and he caught her. "You'd better go back to bed," he whispered.

She nodded. "Yes, silly of me. I'm sorry." He guided her out of the bathroom. She was asleep on her feet.

The agents in the living room were awake, in action, a tape recorder working. Wright demanded to know who was on the line. A young agent in shirtsleeves shook his head. "No need to hear this, Mr. Wright. It's not worth it."

Wright grabbed a stray phone and held it to his ear. A muffled voice, sibilant and unintelligible, as if from a half-lit world: a boy, perhaps an early adolescent, making sounds like a baby. Faint giggling in the background. Wright swore and racked the receiver with a smack.

"You shouldn't have done that, sir. We were trying to trace it."

Wright raised a hand to the back of his neck and kneaded it. "A lot of those calls come in, don't they?"

"Not a lot, but enough. Though usually not this late. We don't bother you with them."

"No ransom demand."

"No, sir. No legitimate one."

"There's not going to be one, is there?"

"Sir, I don't know."

Wright climbed the stairs, made his way back to the bedroom. Merle lay with the sheet sucked to her skin. He pulled up a small wicker chair and slowly collapsed in it. He was sure she was asleep. Sitting in the near-dark he lit a cigarette.

"I miss her," she said, as if their daughter were not missing and maybe dead but merely away for a spell in someone else's care.

He watched her fall back into a semi-sleep and soon went into one himself, waking when his cigarette slid from his fingers. He had not lit the cigarette properly, and it had burnt out. Somebody rapped lightly on the door.

The young agent stood just outside and spoke in a whisper. "We'd like you to listen in on one. This one's different. It isn't a kid, and there's something funny about it."

Wright nearly tripped getting down the stairs, the agent behind him.

"No need to hurry, Mr. Wright. He's not on the line."

"Then how can I listen?"

"We'll play it."

The second agent stood in the living room with a phone in his hand and gestured urgently.

"He's back," the young agent whispered to Wright. "Talk to him and try to keep him on the line."

Wright snatched the phone. For a second he thought the line was dead and stared wildly at the agents. Then he heard the start of a voice, a pause, static, then the whole voice. He listened to the changing textures, one moment rough and whispering, the next tiny and shrill like a small sick animal. None of the words were clear. Wright, frozen, tried to picture the caller, paste a face on him, and he strained for the power to materialize at his side.

"Please, I can't understand you!"

The caller clicked off.

The young agent took the phone from Wright's hand

and cradled it. "Anything at all familiar about the voice?"

Wright shook his head. "No. Did you trace it?"

The other agent, holding two phones, one with an open line to Boston, said, "Maybe."

"The first one came from a pay booth," said the young agent. "North Station."

"Boston?"

"Yes."

Wright shivered.

"They've traced it," said the other agent, putting down one of the phones. "South Station this time."

The young agent checked his watch. "Can't be the same man. He couldn't have made it in time."

"Sure he could've, driving."

"Yes, you're probably right. Little traffic at this hour."

Wright stumbled forth. "Are they going to catch him?"

The young agent steadied him. "Boston PD's doing all it can, sir."

They waited.

The agent with the phone shook his head. "They missed him."

Wright slumped backwards and made his way to a chair but didn't sit in it. He fumbled for a cigarette. He could not stop shivering. "Will he call again?"

"We don't know, sir. We hope so."

Wright managed to light the cigarette. "He almost seemed to be crying."

"Yes, sir. That's what it seemed like."

Wright sat down, his back rigid. "All we can do is wait."

"Yes, sir."

The phone stayed silent.

Paula Aherne was buried in a Ballardville cemetery before a rooted crowd of the curious. Chief Tull, wearing his poplin jacket, eyed them all. Federal agents armed with cameras shot surreptitiously from the hip, and a solitary agent, wandering from stone to stone, occasionally ducking down, fired through a telescopic lens. John Wright stood alone.

The sun seemed too exquisitely bright for a funeral, the sky too startling a blue. The Unitarian minister was doing his best but clearly did not know the person in the coffin. No television crews were near the site because authorities did not want anyone scared away. The district attorney, with Detective Harty flanking him like a bodyguard, remained on the fringe, visible and available to a knot of nearby Boston newspaper reporters, while seemingly oblivious to their presence.

Many of the men in the crowd were those seen and nodded to in the center of town, frequently near the magazine racks in the library and more often on benches in front of Town Hall. Several women wore pinched expressions, as if they bore grudges against the deceased. The numerous students were a quiet lot. Wright stared straight ahead, at the big box, his head as free of thought as he could manage, as the minister's milk-white hand tossed dirt.

Chief Tull, his moist face looming larger than life, the blotches burning, threw an arm around Wright's shoulders. Wright welcomed the weight, the chief's presence. A reporter approached, and the chief stopped him dead with a fierce gesture. Wright slipped on dark glasses.

The chief escorted him over the grass in the direction of the cars, a hand on his arm as if he were in protective custody. The chief wore his heaviest side arm, a .357 Magnum, an ugly weapon but his proudest possession. Wright's steps were labored. Nothing made sense to him: the murder, the funeral, the sunshine. The chief expectorated gently after a rough cough. They were walking on graves.

"You OK, Mr. Wright?"

He nodded, adjusting his glasses.

"I heard about the excitement, that crazy call. I wouldn't put too much stock in it. Sounds like just another kook." The chief's hand shot out. "Watch your step, Mr. Wright."

Wright's eye was fixed on a squirrel spilling down a tree whose branches spurted leaves, birds dashing out of them. He had run away once as a child, briefly, and he remembered eating an ill-made sandwich in the groomed serenity of a cemetery. Later he had watched the nighttime collect each stone and monument. The chief deftly guided him around a metal marker. Despite the sun's heat, Wright felt a frigid draft.

The chief led him to the car, the Cutlass, the snow tires still on it. The sun blazed on the roof. The chief yanked the door open. He wanted Wright to get in and go, but Wright stood with smoke in front of his face. He had lit a cigarette and was staring through the chief.

"Get in your car, Mr. Wright. Drive away so you don't have to talk to anybody."

"What's going to happen now, Chief?"

"A lot, Mr. Wright. You can depend on it."

"What if that man never calls again?"

"I told you, Mr. Wright. That was probably a kook."

Wright was in a fog, but gradually the chief's insistent voice seeped through, along with other voices, people drawing near. He let the chief push him into the Cutlass.

"I'll talk to you later, Mr. Wright. I promise."

The agent with the silver glasses, who looked more like a minister than the Unitarian, remained in place and watched the crowd disperse. He was an impossibly neat man with a pale neutral face and a Teutonic air. Slender hands, no rings. No unnecessary weight. His glasses caught the sun's blare as he nodded at the coffin poised over the hidden hole.

"The answers are in there," he said to the stout agent, "and we're about to bury them."

5

A fixed silence. They were giving him time to think, the two of them seated in the tight quarters before his undersized desk. His name was Oliver, and his office was nearly identical to Wright's, perhaps a shade larger. He had a kind of heavy handsomeness and a full head of prematurely gray hair worn modishly long. He dipped back in his chair.

"It's difficult answering questions about a colleague, but if I had to sum him up, I'd call him a regular guy. As I mentioned, we're not close friends, but what I know of him I like."

The stout agent, who was doing the questioning, said, "Then would you say he's generally well-liked?"

"Let me put it this way. There's a lot of politics at a college, any college. He doesn't play them. There's also a lot of gossips, big-mouths. He's not one of them."

"Is he popular with his students? I mean, as far as you know."

"He's not unpopular."

The stout agent referred to notes or pretended to. "What about Mrs. Wright? What do you know about her?"

"I've met her. Faculty family gatherings, that sort of thing."

"A good-looking woman."

"Yes, extremely. And very pleasant."

The stout agent shuffled his notes, and the silence became fixed again. The agent with the glasses, his arms folded against his chest, was staring at Oliver as if with only minor interest.

"Absolutely horrible what happened," Oliver said, breaking the silence with a soft voice. "How's the investigation going?"

The stout agent, still occupied with his notes, seemed not to hear. The agent with the glasses said, "How old are you, Mr. Oliver?"

"Thirty-five."

The arms casually unfolded. "Thirty-five."

"I know. I look older. The hair."

Silence. Oliver swung forward and toyed with a pencil on his desk. He waggled it suddenly at the agent with the glasses.

"Mind if I ask you something? Were you a lawyer or an accountant? Usually it's one of the two with the FBI, am I right?"

"We prefer to ask the questions, Mr. Oliver."

"Ah," said Oliver with a quick smile. "You're the lawyer, I thought so. And he's the accountant."

The stout agent broke in. "I'll tell you what strikes us odd, Mr. Oliver. You don't remember Paula Aherne at all. You did say that, didn't you?"

Oliver pointed the pencil. "I've been asked that before by your own people and again by that state police detective, whatever his name is. Why am I being asked again?"

"You've had more time to refresh your memory."

The stout agent smiled. "Often time is all it takes."

Oliver sighed impatiently. "As I said before, I might very well have seen this Paula Aherne, might have seen her several times if she monitored my class, as I'm told she did, but I simply don't remember her. Introduction to Psychology, seventy-two students registered, way over what I wanted. You know where I hold the class? The auditorium. See the problem?"

"She never spoke to you?"

"I'd have remembered."

"Very attractive girl."

"I'd have remembered that too."

"Yes," said the agent with the glasses. "That's what we thought."

Oliver sat back. "Ah, comes the light. You fellows have been busy on the campus, and gossip tells you I'm friendly with female students, too friendly perhaps in a few cases. OK. I understand the questions now."

"In an investigation like this," the stout agent said, his notes no longer in sight, "we hear a lot of things. We understand you try to be discreet. We know you have a happy marriage."

"Thank you. That's like a Good Housekeeping seal of approval. Maybe I should frame it and hang it at home. Or would you gentlemen prefer to do it? Give you a chance to chat with my wife and tell her how discreet I've been."

The stout agent appeared hurt. "You're misreading us, Mr. Oliver."

Oliver rocked in his chair. "I'd think the lawyer there would be asking the questions. Why aren't you, sir?"

The agent with the glasses ignored him, even while staring at him. He stopped rocking.

"I wasn't screwing Paula Aherne. That's obviously what you're getting at, isn't it?"

"Again you misread us," the stout agent said.

"I read you fine. Would you like me to give the name of the girl I am screwing and have been since the start of the semester?"

The agent with the glasses rose. "No need. We know."

"Who?" Oliver demanded, as if this were a game, he the student, they the teachers, with a grade at stake. Both agents were now standing, and Oliver sighed wearily, almost with admiration. "You fellows are something."

"The semester ends next week," the stout agent said. "Will you still be available?"

"Yes," Oliver said, staying in his chair.

"Good." The stout agent placed his card on the desk. "Just in case you want to call us."

The agents left.

Oliver reached for the card and shredded it. Then he turned in his chair and gazed out the window at scattered strings of clouds. He felt as if he had flunked a course.

Wright served Merle chicken soup and insisted she eat some. She sat on the edge of the bed in her robe, her hair drawn back, her face hollow and hard. She tasted the soup, a cautious half spoonful.

"Who sent it over?"

"The Harringtons."

"They're good neighbors, good people."

"How's the soup?"

"Good." She had difficulty swallowing. Wright was staring. "I'm all right, really," she said.

He sat back in the wicker chair, his hands flat on his thighs. He had showered and shaved and cut himself.

"How are my parents taking it?" she asked.

"Your father thought it best not to tell your mother, at least not right away."

"How is she?"

"The emphysema's no worse. Your father wanted to fly right out to us, but I told him not to leave her."

"No, he shouldn't." She placed her spoon in the bowl.

"You haven't eaten much."

"Later." She set the soup on the side table. "Is anything happening?" she asked, and he was uncertain how to answer. Before he had a chance, she said, "Is anything *going* to happen?"

He leaned out of the chair. "Merle, she's alive, I know it. I wouldn't say it if I didn't feel it so strongly."

She nodded. "I have to believe that too."

He took her hands and quietly told her about the anonymous caller, sparing the details of the man's ungodly sounds, carefully watching her eyes, which were coming alive.

Her voice lunged. "I want to listen when he calls again."

"He might not. I've been told not to make too much out of it."

"Do you think he has Marcie?"

"I think he was trying to tell me something, but maybe I only wanted to think that."

She touched his face. He had prominent pouches beneath his eyes. She leaned toward him, and he held her in the curve of his arm.

"When you're up to it," he said, "two men would

like to talk with you. No hurry. You don't even have to if you don't want to."

"Who are they?"

He told her.

"I want to."

"You're sure?"

She was on her feet. "Give me time to bathe. Tell them twenty minutes."

He rose and reached for her, embraced her, spoke into her hair. "Merle, I love you."

"I know you do," she said almost inaudibly. "Don't ever stop."

"She'll be down," Wright said, entering the den. The stout agent was seated near the coffee table, which had been Paula Aherne's favorite place to study while minding Marcie. The agent with the glasses sat at the far end of the room, near bookshelves, as if he were only an onlooker.

"How is she?" the stout agent asked as Wright dropped into a leather chair near him.

"Better." Wright lit a cigarette and lay his head back. He heard the distant agent leave his chair and step to the bookshelves. Then the voice:

"What's this about, Mr. Wright?"

Wright brought his head forward. The agent seemed to stand in a thin perfectly straight line. "I can't see it," Wright said, squinting. The agent raised the book, an oversized paperback, the cover a flash of black and white; woman, sun, bird.

"I think the victim had a copy in her room," the stout agent prompted in a whisper, as if he and Wright were on one side and the other agent on another.

Wright raised his voice. "It's about a man looking

into his new life from the perspective of his old one. He had much grief in his old life. He lost his mother, wife, and daughter."

The agent with the glasses silently slid the book back into its place. "I wonder if that's what she did."

"Did what?" Wright's throat was sore, and he put out the cigarette. He looked back toward the gleam of glasses.

"I wonder whether we become what we read, Mr. Wright."

"Very likely. In varying degrees."

"She lied to you, Mr. Wright. Do you bear her a grudge?"

"How can I bear her a grudge? She's dead." He turned to the stout agent. "Anything yet on the man who made those calls?"

"I'm afraid not."

"No fingerprints?"

"Hundreds. Don't get your hopes up on that one, Mr. Wright. Even if we get him, it could be a dead end."

Merle entered the room, her dark hair pulled hard around her skull, her face touched with a little makeup. The stout agent stood while Wright gave her the leather chair and then sat on the arm.

"Thanks for coming down, Mrs. Wright. How are you feeling?" She nodded, and the agent resumed his place, producing a gold pen and small notebook from his suitcoat. "This won't take long, I promise. Your husband's been very helpful, but you spent more time with Miss Aherne. You're aware she made up things about her background."

"My husband told me."

"Have you any idea why she did that?"

"They didn't seem like lies. Now, looking back, more like fairy tales."

"Yes, that's interesting. But what concerns us now is anything that'll help us learn who she really was. We need some place to start."

"Boston."

"Boston's a big place, Mrs. Wright, and there's no record she ever lived there, though she may well have. Any places in Boston she might've mentioned?"

Merle was silent for several seconds. "She spoke of an Italian coffee bar in the North End. She spoke of it only once, but it seemed terribly special to her." She glanced swiftly up at Wright. "Do you remember my telling you?"

"Yes, and I've already mentioned it to them." He placed a hand on her shoulder, which was faintly trembling.

"Your husband also mentioned dating bars?"

"Yes. She said she didn't like them, didn't care for that kind of crowd."

"She mention any in particular?"

"I don't know. No, I don't think so."

"Well, what brought up the subject?"

"I don't remember."

"Please think hard on that, Mrs. Wright. A place that might have especially distressed her."

Merle nervously shifted her weight and noticed for the first time the presence of the other agent, who was sharply observing her from his chair across the room. "No, I'm sorry," she said.

The stout agent doodled odd circles in his notebook, a cluster of eyes, nose and mouth, a shapeless face, a ghost on paper, as if for Merle to see. "I'm not going to keep you any longer, Mrs. Wright. I know how trying this is, but if you should think of anything else, no matter how small, please let us know."

"My daughter."

"We're doing everything we can."

The other agent had silently left his chair and now stood near the coffee table, as if intruding only because he had to. "Mrs. Wright, why didn't you ask the girl for references?"

The dry voice startled her. "We were going to. We forgot. Then it didn't seem necessary."

"Yes, I understand."

Wright rose from the arm of the chair. "You asked me that two or three days ago. Don't you remember?"

"Yes, of course."

The stout agent interjected: "You probably explained it to me, Mr. Wright, and I forgot to pass it on. Sorry."

Merle spoke out of a blank face: "She wouldn't have hurt Marcie. She would've fought to protect her."

The stout agent slowly put away his pen and notebook.

Merle rose, as if she could no longer bear to sit. "Would you gentlemen like coffee? I'm going to make some."

They politely declined. She left the room, and Wright stood still. The agent with the glasses had drifted back. He was looking toward Wright but with his chin tilted, as if his interest were well beyond.

"I hope we didn't upset her," the stout agent said. "How is she really, Mr. Wright?"

"She's coming out of it. She's going to be all right."

"How about you, Mr. Wright?"

"Yes, I'm all right." Wright looked toward the door. "Would you excuse me?"

"Just one more thing, for my own information." The agent's voice dipped. "That book you were talking about—heavy reading? Would the girl have needed help understanding it?"

"I wouldn't think so," Wright said and stepped by.

Merle stood by the stove, no coffee being made. Her lips barely moved. "They're making us feel guilty."

"It's their way," he said.

"Maybe we are guilty."

"Merle, don't."

Her voice rose. "You haven't thought about it?"

"Yes, of course, but—"

"You and I, John. We're to blame. I more than you."

"No."

"Yes!"

He put a gentle hand to her face because he thought she might scream.

She merely flinched.

The district attorney's office in the Essex County Court building was institutionally plain, with the drapes on the single window the only extravagance. One small wall was taken with photographs of the DA with various visiting politicians, all Democrats, including the surviving Kennedy.

"Thanks for coming, Chief."

"Thanks for asking me," Chief Tull said. He sat directly before the DA's desk, his poplin jacket open, one leg slung over the other. The DA's young assistant sat on the chief's distant left, primly like a secretary, and Detective Harty sat on the chief's immediate right. The detective glanced down at the chief's side.

"Quite a cannon you've got there."

The chief smiled.

"Ever fire it at anybody?" Harty asked.

"No, never have," the chief said with another smile. "But there's always the first time."

The DA, making himself more comfortable behind his desk, said to Harty, "Why don't you begin."

The detective straightened, and his voice rose. "We still don't know if the kid's alive or dead, but each day goes by makes it more likely she's dead, which has been my belief from the start. A double homicide."

The chief slowly shook his head.

"You disagree, Chief?" the DA asked.

"No, no, go on. I'm just listening."

The detective shifted his weight. "What screws everything up is the dead sitter. We still don't know a damned thing about her, and I'm pretty sure the Feds haven't come up with anything either."

"What about the Feds?" the DA asked insinuatingly.

"They make a show of sharing, but that's all it is, a show. Anyway, by now her picture's probably been all over the country and back, and we haven't gotten any responses that have led anywhere. She never had an aunt that worked at Sears, that's for sure, and we've checked every Aherne in metropolitan Boston and have come up with zero. Plenty of people have been killed on the Southeast Expressway but none who could've been her parents. Plenty of kids at the college saw her around, talked to her, but none really knew her. Only people who had any real contact with her were the Wrights."

"What about the Wrights?" the DA asked.

"We've checked them out right down to the movie they saw that night, and a waitress at Brigham's remembered them. They're OK."

"What was the movie they saw? X-rated?"

"It was PG, I forget the name. I've got it somewhere."

The chief spoke up. "They're good people, you can take my word for it."

The DA grinned. "I hear the wife's got nice legs."

"Nice everything," the detective said.

"They're a nice couple," the chief said, stirring uncomfortably.

The DA folded his arms and said to the detective, "They married kind of late, didn't they? Means they probably both had been around. You talk to her yet?"

"Feds beat me to it. But like I said, they both seem straight. No history of mental trouble, no therapy sessions, no odd behavior."

The DA dropped his arm and placed a hand on his desk. "So let's get back to the sitter. You know what we have there, don't you? A phantom in death. That's what the *Herald-American* called her. Did you see the story?"

The detective nodded. "I've got computer printouts, photographs, and reports all over my office, all from inquiries about missing persons throughout the country, particularly runaways. All negative."

"She could've been a hustler," the DA said. "That three hundred dollars didn't come from nowhere."

"I suppose," said the detective, "we can speculate all day whether her real identity had anything to do with what happened to her and the kid. It's pretty hard to discount it. On the other hand, it could've been a simple B and E that turned into something else. Let's say the guy, probably flying high, bumps into the sitter, panics and pops her. Let's say this guy likes his kicks a mile a minute, which makes the baby a bonus, the prize in the Crackerjacks, something to take away to play with in private and later dump, bury or whatever. We've been checking people out on that score, but so far nothing."

The DA was silent, and so was the chief.

"Whether it happened that way or not," the detective said, "I still believe the kid is dead."

"No, she's not," the chief said in a rugged tone, and all eyes went to him.

"Why do you say that, Chief?" the DA asked.

"It's a feeling I've got."

The DA and the detective exchanged glances. The DA patted his gut. "Is this where you've got it, Chief?"

"Yes."

The DA shifted back to the detective. "If this was a double homicide and not a real kidnaping, we don't need the Feds around, do we?" He made his eyes small. "But we've got to come up with the body."

The chief slouched in his chair and did not listen to the detective's response.

"They're not going to find anything," the chief muttered. He and the young officers stood near an edge of the forest, part of a state reservation shared by three towns. State troopers and a horde of volunteers had penetrated the Ballardville section. "They're wasting their time."

"Never can tell, Chief."

The officer's cap looked unsteady on his overgrowth of hair, which substantially increased the disdain in the slow look the chief gave him.

"Take my word for it, OK?"

The sun was brilliant and the sky pure except for a few small clouds laid out as if in code. The cool scent of the woods was strong.

"Look at that!" the officer said, pointing to a scrap of color fluttering high in an oak. "That's an oriole. You'll see his mate in a minute."

The chief viewed him with more disdain. "You know birds?"

"Sure. I grew up with them. My mother was a fancier."

The chief vaguely suspected a put-on and turned away.

"Wait a minute, Chief. The mate will show up."

"Come on!"

The chief walked on the road, with the officer catching up, the two of them in a fast smart step as if in close-order drill, past a long stretch of cars parked on the shoulder. The road shimmered with illusions of water. The chief's car was at the very end, pointed in the wrong way. It was dark blue, with the town seal imprinted on each side and "Police" painted on the trunk. The chief usually drove himself, but sometimes, for show, he made a chauffeur out of an officer while he sat in back.

The car was hot, no breeze, no air-conditioning, only open windows. The officer waited with splayed fingers on the wheel, his eyes in the rearview. The chief said nothing.

"Where to?" the officer finally asked.

"Nowhere till I say."

The chief seemed to be losing himself in thought. The officer removed his cap, hunched forward, and peered through the windshield. A scattering of small forest birds hovered in the sky like scratches on a chart. The officer sat back with a loud sigh.

"We just going to sit here, Chief?"

"Right. Till I say different."

The officer's eyes flitted back to the rearview. "Aren't you hot in that jacket, Chief?"

No answer. The officer pulled a package of Kents out of his pocket and started to light up.

"Don't smoke!"

The officer threw the cigarette out and stared hard at the forest, as if envying those in it.

"I hope that butt was out," the chief said.

"Yes, sir, it was." The officer mopped his forehead and twisted around. "Chief, I'm roasting."

So was the chief. He seemed to be burning up, his blotches flaming, sweat streaming down his cheeks. He was, however, smiling.

"I'm remembering something."

"What is it, Chief?"

"Back in March or April, that's when it was."

"What?"

The chief flung open the door, leaped out, and yanked at the driver's door. "Shove over!"

The radial tires screeched, blew up gravel and burnt tar as the chief made a one-hundred-eighty-degree turn, the wheel almost spinning out of his hands. Then it was full speed ahead, siren wailing.

6

In a shadowy room at the Ballardville Motor Inn, located near an entrance to Route 93, Oliver lay with a student, a full-blown woman of eighteen with cascading hair and freckles. The sheet tossed aside, she leaned over him and measured him with metaphors meant to tease him, to flatter him one moment and diminish him the next. "Timber," she said in a husky voice, "twig" in a small one.

His eyes were closed, his face unresponsive.

"Tusk," she said. "Tooth. Hey, I like that. Has anyone ever called it a tooth?"

He was uneasy. He had wanted to leave as soon as they had broken from their embrace and now was waiting only for a decent interval.

She kissed his ear and whispered, "What does your wife call it?"

He reacted strongly, more than he meant to, and she pulled away and viewed him sardonically.

"Oh, I see. Sorry. I'm not supposed to ask about that."

He raised an apologetic hand, but she avoided the touch. She hopped off the bed, which was what he had wanted but not that way. She glared at him.

"I don't need you, you know. I don't have you for anything now."

He stared at her as if disappointed in her and in himself. He liked her—a little more than she probably thought. He sat up, smoothing his hair back, and said, "I'm sorry. It's just that I've got a lot on my mind."

"Sure."

She snatched up her scant underpants and put them on. Usually she'd have showered first, he with her. He watched her throw on a green blouse the shade and shine of holly. Her fingers flew from button to button. He swung his legs and stood up with a bounce. She turned her back and stepped into a flowing skirt, which was hand-made, her hand, her design. He went to her.

"If you don't mind!"

He drew back and dressed quickly while she fixed her hair in the bathroom, taking more time than necessary, perhaps to calm her anger. He smiled when she reappeared with brushed hair.

"Friends?"

"Sure," she said, but her voice was cold.

They left the room together, he with a briefcase, as if it were luggage. The sunlight in the parking lot was a blast, and the heat was intense. There was a car near his, improperly parked, two shapes in it, silhouettes that seemed surreal because of the violent sun-splash across the windshield. Oliver stopped in his tracks.

"Wait a minute."

"What's the matter?"

"Wait here."

He took fast strides, his briefcase swinging, and he wasn't absolutely sure who they were until he reached the passenger side and dipped at the waist, placing a hand on the ledge of the open window.

"What do you want?"

Glasses glinted at him, and he dropped his hand because it was shaking, as much from rage as from fear, at first a very rational fear and then a silly one that they might drug him, drag him away, and rummage through his briefcase. He instantly tightened his grip on it, even though it contained nothing but old student papers.

"What are you doing here?"

The agent with the glasses said nothing, as if no explanation were needed. The other agent, relaxed behind the wheel, seemed to be gazing out at the young woman, who had stayed in place.

"Do you want to speak to me?"

"No," said the agent with the glasses. "Do you want to speak to us?"

Oliver staggered back a bit. "Look, don't do this to me!"

"Do what, sir?"

Oliver straightened, got hold of himself, and returned to the young woman, who appeared puzzled and amused. She smiled.

"Who are they—private detectives? Maybe your wife's not so dumb after all."

"Come on!" he said, tearing at her arm. His car was a red Pinto Runabout with white markings. He had an urge to burn rubber and roar past the offending faces. Instead he backed the Pinto up carefully, turned it about, and slowly rolled by the other car as if he'd lost all interest in the occupants.

"We can't meet anymore," he said when they reached the road, and she laughed.

"Yes, I gathered that. Should I expect trouble, maybe a summons?"

He shook his head. "There won't be any trouble."

"What about a call from your wife?"

"She won't call."

"OK, but if she does. I'll tell her it was all a lark. Didn't mean a thing."

He gave her a quick glance and said nothing. With an eye in the rearview he sped to the place where he usually dropped her off.

Chief Tull sat with the Wrights at the kitchen table and opened an envelope of small glossy photographs, about a dozen, which he shuffled through fast to make sure they were all there. He handed them to Wright.

"If you don't mind, I'd like you folks to look at them separate. Take your time and let me know if you've ever seen any of these fellows in the neighborhood. If they are familiar at all."

Wright looked at the first, the second, and then quickly at others. "Some of these you've shown me before."

"Yes, that's right." The chief had arrived mildly excited and now seemed more so. "But you weren't yourself then, Mr. Wright, and your wife hasn't seen any of them yet."

Wright started fresh, studying each mug shot with care. He had been shown so many lately, particularly by the husky detective, that the faces were beginning to look alike. Finally he shook his head, and the chief fell forward.

"I had a few new ones. Did you notice?"

"Which ones?"

The chief quickly pointed them out and waited with noticeable anticipation, but again Wright shook his head.

"Would you look at them, Mrs. Wright?"

Merle pounced upon them, separated them like playing cards, and tried to look at them all at once. Amazingly she seemed to do just that. Then she went through them one at a time, more slowly than her husband had, each picture upsetting her because none was familiar and all were frightening. One made her flinch, that of a curly-haired man with hooded eyes and scarcely any lips. The chief leaped from his chair but sank slowly back when Merle shook her head.

Wright, his face edged with suspicion, said, "Chief, are you holding anything back?"

The chief unzipped his poplin jacket, as if prepared to stay for a while. "I don't want to raise your hopes too soon, and I was hoping you might come up with something on those pictures."

"Chief, what is it?"

"I think I'm on to something, but it's too soon to tell."

"Tell me," Wright said, trying to keep anger out of his impatience. Merle moved to the edge of her chair. The chief sat back in his.

"It was in the back of my mind all this time. Parker Street. Where Paula Aherne lived."

"Yes!"

"Parker Street. Parker Street. All along it kept nagging me, something about that street, and then I remembered. I went to the station, to the log, and it hit me right in the eye. April twenty-first, a Friday, a complaint logged at 9:32 P.M. You see I read that log every day, religiously, and that's how I remembered."

"Chief, please."

"Nine-thirty-two P.M., this old lady who lives across the street from Paula Aherne's rooming house calls in to say some man's been standing a good half-hour in the dark near her lilacs, not doing anything, just standing there. So an officer responds, but by the time he gets there—maybe he was in no big hurry, I don't know—the guy's gone. The old lady can't give a description since it's dark and his back was turned. The officer figures she's batty but gives a look-around with the flashlight. Nothing. Checks back later. Nothing."

"What does it mean?"

"She said his back was turned to her, and that means he was looking straight at the rooming house."

"Who is he?" Merle asked in a tone that demanded a name.

"Mrs. Wright, I don't know yet. I've got men talking to everybody on the street, but it looks like the old lady—Mrs. Nelligan's her name—was the only one to see him."

"Is she batty?" Wright asked.

"I don't think so, I really don't."

"April twenty-first," Merle said. "That was two weeks before it happened."

"I know."

"And you think it has a bearing."

"I do, Mrs. Wright. I've got a very good feeling about it."

Merle rose. "I'll get you some coffee."

"No, none for me, thank you." The chief packed away the photographs and got to his feet. Wright walked him to the door. The hallway walls had been repapered. Wright had called a man in to do it. There was a new rug on the floor. The chief stepped back for a look into the living room.

"Hey, where are the federal boys?"

"Gone, but they're keeping a tap on the phone."

The chief nodded slowly. "No more calls from that freaky fellow?"

"No."

"You know, that could tie in to my man. Well, we'll see."

"Chief, please keep in touch."

"You and your wife can count on it," he said, as if their lives were sewn to his.

Wright closed the front door quietly and returned to Merle, who had gotten out the can of coffee but had not proceeded from there. Her smile was pained.

"He's trying so hard," she said.

Wright nodded. "I know."

"But he doesn't seem to be getting anywhere. None of them do."

"I'll make the coffee," Wright said.

She held him. "John, if they can't get anywhere, can we?"

"I don't know, but I think we'd better try."

They embraced with a chaste touch of lips.

Oliver and the stout agent met in a luncheonette in downtown Ballardville and took a back booth. The agent ordered the breakfast special, and Oliver, haggard after a bad night, asked for only coffee.

"Where's your buddy? The lawyer."

The agent smiled. "You don't need the both of us, do you?"

"I want the both of you off my back."

The agent sighed, as if he deserved better.

"Tell me what you want," Oliver said, jolting forward, trying to keep his voice down. "Am I a suspect or something?"

"Don't get us wrong, Mr. Oliver."

"Just answer my question, if you don't mind."

The waitress returned, and the agent made a quieting gesture, as if his main concern were for Oliver's welfare whether Oliver chose to believe that or not. "Ah, thank you," he said to the waitress and spread a small inadequate napkin over his lap. He ate eggs, ate them without looking up, as if performing a rush task, again for Oliver's benefit.

Oliver creamed and sugared his coffee but barely touched it, glancing furtively at other customers, most of them perched with their backs to him at the counter but with their faces visible in the length of mirror. Several were town hall workers, whom he considered great little gossips, and he wished now he had chosen a different time or place to meet with the agent.

"Not bad," the agent said, raising the napkin to his mouth and reaching for his coffee. "Take my toast if you want. I doubt that I'll eat it."

"I don't want your toast. I want to know what I have to do to get you off my back."

The agent sipped his coffee and shook his head like a man much misunderstood; yet he was almost smiling, as if enjoying the situation. Oliver twisted in his seat and sat sideways, crossing his legs under the table. Lowering his voice considerably, he said, "You obviously think I might have murdered that girl and stolen the baby."

"Oh, my God, Mr. Oliver. Don't say that."

Oliver's chin shot up. "What are you, the good guy and the lawyer's the bad one?"

The agent casually put his cup down. "Did you ever consider this might be as unpleasant for us as for you? Perhaps, though, I have a solution. You certainly know what a polygraph is."

Oliver exhaled noisily. "You want me to take one."

"Do you mind?"

"I have a choice?"

"Certainly do."

"I don't get this. Mine wasn't the only class that girl monitored. What about the other teachers? Are you going to subject them to lie detectors?"

"The other teachers remembered her."

"So what?"

"Maybe the polygraph will stir your memory."

"A polygraph proves nothing."

"But it disproves things. It takes people such as you off the hook. Isn't that what we're after?"

Oliver smiled thinly. "Why do I feel I'm being set up? OK, when?"

"Tomorrow morning. I'll pick you up at nine."

"I don't want you picking me up at my home."

"You tell me."

"Right here. No, make it in front of the library. Right down the street."

"Fine."

The agent left the tip and paid the check. Oliver headed briskly toward his Pinto, parked near the bank, and the agent strolled in the opposite direction, picking up his pace after rounding the corner. He climbed into the driver's side of a sedan. The agent with the glasses folded the newspaper and laid it to one side.

"How did it go?"

"Fine," the stout agent said, rubbing his hands as if for circulation. "He played it exactly the way he should. Just dumb enough and just smart enough. I think he's one hell of a smooth fellow."

"Ride this road much?" the stout agent asked, traveling at a good clip in the Route 93 traffic, keeping to the outside lane, at times tailgating a car to move it over. Oliver, sitting beside him, shook his head.

"Only when my wife and I go to Boston, which isn't that much."

"I guess teaching keeps you pretty busy," the agent said with a sideways glance. " 'Course you take the summers off, which is nice. Are you a professor?"

"Just an instructor," Oliver said, his mind numbed by the monotony of the ride and his stomach unsettled by the anticipation of the polygraph. He tried to tuck away time by counting cars they passed and saw a Pinto that looked like his. He wished he were in it.

The Boston skyline loomed ahead.

The agent, whistling a song from the forties, began shifting lanes, edging toward the second Somerville exit, which confused Oliver. He gave the agent a stricken glance.

"I thought we were going into Boston, the Federal Building or wherever."

"No, I'm sorry. I thought I told you, and I guess I didn't. My mistake. We're going into Cambridge. MIT."

"MIT? Why?"

"There's a fellow there who's a real expert, one of the very best, and his equipment is super. This is for your benefit."

Oliver closed his eyes for a moment.

"Everything OK?" the agent asked.

"Yes, of course."

"Don't be nervous. I'll tell you something about machines. They don't lose their touch as fast as a man does. I used to be able to size people up with a glance. Now I need a lot more time."

Oliver looked away. The agent took a fast turn before Lechmere Square, cut down streets nearly boxed in by parked cars, and made his way along the back route to the Massachusetts Institute of Technology, a formidable smoke-colored complex of new architecture blocked into the old, its appearance more governmental than collegiate, more military than civilian.

The agent left the car in a huge lot, and he and Oliver followed an asphalt path. Oliver kept his eyes straight ahead and saw little and took note of nothing, not even the name of the building they entered. The agent led the way up wide stairs to a second-floor corridor lined with doors, some open, most not. The agent with the glasses and another man were waiting for them at one of the distant doors, which was closed. The agent with the glasses stepped forward.

"Thank you for coming, Mr. Oliver. This gentleman will try not to keep you too long."

Oliver stared at the stranger, who was short and slight and had a frugal face and a neat close beard. Oliver forced a smile. "Are you FBI or MIT, or doesn't it make a difference anymore?"

"Just somebody doing a job, sir," the man said, unlocking the door and holding it open.

Oliver hesitated. The agents had withdrawn and were in conversation with each other. Oliver looked down at his shoes, shined for the occasion. Stepping past the man, he breathed in sharply and made his stomach flat and inflexible, as if to withstand a punch from the polygraph.

7

John and Merle Wright, convinced that Paula Aherne's hidden identity was the only link to their daughter, drove into Boston with no definite plan, no mental map, and were immediately caught in convulsive traffic on the Central Artery. The clogged artery spanned the business edge of the city and put the Wrights in touch with only the tops and backs of buildings and with a clock that wasn't telling the right time.

"Can you get off this?"

"I'm trying," Wright said, glancing fast over his shoulder for a chance to jolt the Cutlass into the next lane. Merle lit a cigarette and immediately put it out.

"God, I'm smoking too much. That's all I do."

"Give me one."

A cigarette in his mouth and the smoke smarting his eyes, Wright ignored a blasting horn and swerved toward the Haymarket off-ramp, braking once and then gunning it. He headed toward Quincy Market and then angled away from it because of the traffic, worsened by the pile and push of pedestrians.

"Relax," Merle said, touching him.

"You, too."

"We could try Sears," she said. "Maybe talk to the clerks."

He flipped away the cigarette. "By now the police have been to every Sears in the state. That was one of Paula's lies."

"All right, where then?"

"I'm thinking," he said, slowing for lights near the South Station and peering at the massive stone building, part fortress, part cathedral. "That's where he called from the second time, the last time."

"Do you want to go in?"

"We don't even know which phone booth."

"John, we've got to start somewhere."

"Not there."

When the lights broke, he drove straight past the station and skirted the wharf area, slicing smoothly through traffic that was only sporadically heavy now, hitting the lights right and gliding past the Army Base and a foreign ship in the harbor, the ship near enough to distinguish faces of seamen meandering the deck. The breeze off the water was a gift.

"I know where you're going," Merle said. "What do you think you're going to find there?"

"I don't know."

He made an abrupt turn, sailed along for a while, and then hit the lights wrong. They were in the heart of South Boston, an indirect route to where they were going. A teenager pulled up beside them, his car full of rock music. He smiled insinuatingly at Merle, who smiled back, like a mother.

Wright made too many turns, confused by narrow one-way streets and often confounded by irregularly parked cars. He scraped a derelict Dodge wagon, and a man sitting on a stoop hollered, "Go head, take it home with you!"

Merle edged closer to him. "Easy, John."

"We're all right now," he said, taking his next left.

"What are we going to do there?"

He hunched his shoulders.

"I don't know Dorchester that well," she said. "You don't either."

"I used to."

"John, that was years ago."

"Trust me."

But he soon saw he shouldn't have trusted himself. Street signs were twisted out of shape and threw him off course. Landmarks he expected were not there, and the single-family houses he remembered had been turned into tenements. The faces in the windows and from the sidewalks were black, which brought him up short, for he had never associated blacks in Boston with any section other than Roxbury. The traffic was stop-and-go, with youths weaving through it on foot.

"Roll up your window," he said, cranking his, then striking the door lock.

"I'm not frightened."

"Please, play it safe," he said and reached past her to hit the button on her door.

Six youths splitting three to a side approached the Cutlass, brushing against it, trailing fingers and staring silently through the glass. Merle looked straight ahead, and Wright from the corner of his eye saw a pair of pink palms on his window. The palms slipped away, and an amused brown face blotted the glass.

"Hey, mister. You've got a dent."

Wright acknowledged the voice and tried to match

the grin. Then he eased the Cutlass forward, flashed the directional, and took the next turn, a congested street and an endless thicket of tenement houses, mostly four-decker. Merle lowered the window.

"She didn't live here, John."

"We haven't found her street yet."

She put a hand on his leg. "She never lived in Dorchester. I simply know it. OK?"

Wright covered her hand with his. "One thing we've got to realize, Merle. We never knew her."

"John, take my word for it. She didn't live here. I don't *hear* her. No whispers. No echoes."

Wright gave her a glance at once curious and tender. "That's about all we have to go on, isn't it? Intuition."

She nodded. "For a while."

She was quiet, and he headed back toward a more familiar Boston, pale in the heat, the only exception the Hancock, a blue blade of a building, a slice in the haze. He set his eye on the Hancock, but felt himself shifting away from it, as if something were guiding him, and he realized it was Merle's hand, freed from his and pointing the way, as if the city were a vast Ouija board.

"Where are we going?" he asked.

"I don't know." She had tears in her eyes.

"Where would you like to go?"

She turned to him, eyes glistening. "Maybe I do have intuition. Maybe I can *feel* my way to Marcie. Why shouldn't I be able to? She came out of my flesh?"

Wright slipped an arm around her and drove one-handed down Charles Street, between the Boston Common and the Public Garden. "Tell me where you want to go," he said gently.

"The North End," she said without hesitation.

"The Italian coffee bar?"

"Yes."

He followed Charles Street to the rotary and hooked a sharp right onto Cambridge Street, breezing past the drab side of Beacon Hill. Merle's hand went to his wrist.

"John, I'm only guessing."

"Maybe not," he said.

Chief Tull, his hair reddish in the sunshine and his face more blotched than usual, cut the Wrights' grass. He decided to do it when he didn't find them at home and saw dandelions consuming the lawn. He dragged the power mower from the unlocked garage, hung his poplin jacket in the red maple and, with his weapon still holstered to his hip, did the front first. By the time he reached the back he was panting.

He stripped to the waist, hanging the sweat-soaked shirt in the oak, and he placed his naked Magnum in a pocket of roots. The back was rougher to do, uneven ground, flower beds to worry about, and the sun seemed more intense and was certainly lively on his skin. He paused once to refuel the mower and to refresh himself with the lawn hose and a second time to let a pain in his side pass. He was working the mower over a hump when he felt eyes from afar. Mrs. Harrington, kerchiefed and in garden gloves, was standing near her white roses and giving him a long inquisitive stare, which immediately took away some of the fun he was having.

Growing careless as his satisfaction soured by the second, he lightened his grip on the mower, and a bed of red flowers flew up like flames, which distressed him. He did not want to hurt anything that belonged to the

Wrights. He gave a quick glance toward Mrs. Harrington to see whether she had witnessed the destruction, and it was obvious she had, though she was turning her back to him. As he began pushing harder to get the job done faster, his face lowered to his chest, the pain in his side returned, sharper than before and longer lasting, and he noticed with alarm that his head was humming.

He killed the mower and stood in place waiting for his breath, his chest heaving and his eyes half closed, the sun spraying him. He did not see the heavy figure approaching from the far side of the house until it was upon him.

"What the hell you doing, Chief?"

The chief jerked his head and saw Harty from the DA's office. "What's it look like?" he said, trying to hide embarrassment as the detective's eyes slowly swept him.

"Jesus, I don't know, but I hope you're getting paid for it." Harty let a smile creep out. "You've got an empty holster there. Didn't lose anything, did you?"

"My piece is locked in the trunk of my car. Don't worry about it."

Harty glanced toward the other yard and whispered. "That broad over there's got her eye on you. Must be your muscles." The chief did not respond, and Harty widened his smile. "Chief, I am worried about you because you're burning up. Look at your shoulders. Rosier than a nipple on a good girl's tit. What the hell you doing this for?"

The chief glared through his sweat and said, "Too much for you to understand." He bent down and disconnected the mower's spark plug, burning his fingers and sucking the one that hurt worse. It tasted of gasoline. Then he began pushing the mower toward the garage.

"Hey, Chief. You didn't finish."

He kept going. He wheeled the mower into a corner and stood by it, relishing the cool of the garage and letting his skin soak in the damp. He was nursing his fingers when the detective appeared in the doorway.

"You forgot these, Chief." Harty held up the shirt and the Magnum.

The chief emerged from his corner like a tired fighter, snatched his belongings, and strode out of the garage, snaring his jacket from the maple on his way to the car.

"Chief, where are the Wrights?"

"How the hell do I know?" he said without looking back.

"I'm sorry," the bearded man said.

The agent with the glasses shook his head in disgust. "What are you saying? He was smart?"

"No, I'm simply saying he wasn't a good subject. It was inconclusive. Chalk it up to bad body chemistry."

"Can you try again?"

"Sure, but let's wait a week." The bearded man lit a pipe and drew hard on it, while the agent stared at the wall.

"The voice readings were a bust too."

The bearded man puffed and said, "Well, you didn't expect much there, did you? That was a long shot trying to match him with that telephone voice, if you want to call it a voice, more like a dog whimpering. And you had a bad tape to boot, and Ma Bell's static."

The agent shifted his eyes. "When's the last time you had a dud polygraph like this one?"

"It wasn't so long ago, but that was an exceptional subject. He turned out to be clinically schizophrenic."

"Well, what do you think? Maybe this one is."

The bearded man smiled through his smoke. "I doubt it."

The coffee bar was cool and good-smelling, long and cozy, pleasantly crowded with regulars and many tourists, camera-equipped strays from the Freedom Trail and the North End's narrowly twisting streets that bumped into one another in odd places. John and Merle Wright, who had been lucky to find a table, waited for the proprietor's return and the resumption of their conversation with him. Merle craned her neck, her eyes sweeping over a table of Waspish women loading up on cannoli.

"He's still busy," she said.

"Or pretending to be," said Wright. "I don't know what to make of him."

"I don't think he knows what to make of us," she said, settling back with her coffee.

Wright lit a cigarette. "I don't know. We're drawing different impressions of him. I saw absolutely no surprise when we told him who we were, almost as if he were expecting us."

"He was being polite."

"Too polite."

Merle leaned forward. "Somebody's staring at us."

The stare came from a distant waiter, a handsome young man with a fallen slice of raven-black hair hanging down one cheek. His raspberry shirt was open to his chest, and his black pants were stamped to his skin. He shifted his eyes when Wright looked his way.

"I'd bet he's a hand-kisser," Merle whispered.

"And he'd be in your underarm in a second. He's atmosphere, here for the ladies."

"Are we wasting our time?"

"I say we stick it out."

The proprietor made his way toward them, smiling generously at customers, patting the head of a blond boy who had spumoni on his chin, weaving neatly between tiny tables. He was short, heavy, and muscular, with a surprisingly nimble step and a subtle range of smiles that so far had told the Wrights little. He sat at their table with the air of a busy man, laying down heavy hands curled nearly into fists, as if all his strength were concentrated there. He was still smiling.

"Sorry I took so long. Busy time."

"We appreciate the time you're giving us," Wright said, trying to reassess him, re-examining his face, which was made interesting by a drooping left eyelid. The eyes were more black than brown, with a liquid look. His hair was dull iron-gray.

"You have a nice place," Merle said.

He gave out a short appreciative laugh. "Lot of blood and sweat made it that way. My father opened up fifty years ago. His specialty was cannoli and pasticiotti, the best in Boston. Special recipes. Paid a thousand bucks for them to the family of a dying man named Scamporino. My father paid it off a little at a time, and this is what we got."

"Is your father still alive?" Merle asked.

The proprietor blessed himself. "No."

Wright lighted a fresh cigarette.

"Shouldn't smoke so much, friend. You're not doing yourself any good."

Wright set his coffee cup to one side. "Could we get back to Paula Aherne? Was that the name you knew her by?"

"Look, friend, I can understand what you're going through, but I've had federal and state guys here asking me the same things. I can't tell you people any more than I told them, and like I said, you got me at a bad time."

"Please," said Merle, gripping her empty cup.

The proprietor slid his hands together, interlocking the fingers, and appeared to be weighing the alternative of asking them to leave. With a sigh, he turned his eyes back to Wright. "I never knew her last name. Paula is all she called herself, and I'll tell you what I told them. That drawing they showed me didn't really look like her. I mean, I had to study it, you know? It showed her with short hair, and the girl that used to come here had long hair."

"But it was the same girl, wasn't it?"

"Yeah, I guess so. There was a resemblance, but like I said, I had to look for it."

"What did she do when she came here?" Merle asked.

"Hey, you want more coffee?"

Merle shook her head.

"What did she do? She usually sat over there, table by the espresso machine, always by herself, always with a book. You know, one of the paperbacks. Not the dirty kind. She wasn't that kind of kid."

"How do you know that?" Wright asked.

"You get a feel for people. She'd been coming in here maybe almost a year, you know, off and on. And she talked nice, not like something off the streets."

"So you talked to her."

"Sure, I'd say hi and ask how she was doing, stuff like that. She was the quiet type. She came in here for coffee and to read her book. Sometimes she got some of the sesame-seed cookies. You people ought to take some home with you. I'll give you some."

"She ever talk about herself?" Wright asked.

"Never."

Wright snuffed out his cigarette. "What about the waiters? They ever talk to her?"

"Like I did, no more, if that."

"She was a pretty girl."

"You asking if they made a play for her? I don't allow none of that stuff here. This is a place a guy can bring his family. Lots do."

Wright was running out of questions, and he lit another cigarette, his hand slightly shaking.

Merle said, "When did she stop coming here?"

The proprietor unlocked his hands and removed them from the table. "I don't know exactly. Sometime last fall, don't ask me what month."

"I wonder," said Wright, "why she picked this place to read her book."

"Friend. Take a look around. A lot of people pick this place."

"You have no idea where she lived?"

"Never asked."

"Could it have been here in the North End?"

The proprietor smiled. "No way. Nobody lives in the North End without everybody else knowing it."

"Then you really don't know anything about her," Merle said in a discouraged voice, and the proprietor's expression immediately softened.

"Lady, I wish I could help you, I swear to God."

"Thank you. I know you do."

"Look, I can't sit here anymore, but let me get you that bag of cookies, some cannoli too."

They watched him go, saw him gesture fiercely at a waiter to tend to a distant table. Then he seemed to dissolve. Merle's eyes were wet. She wiped them and gazed toward the espresso machine and the table near it. The table was occupied by three persons.

"What do you think?" Wright asked.

"I almost wish we hadn't come," Merle said.

"There was something defensive about him, something that didn't ring right."

"What?"

"I'm not sure. Maybe it was the way he talked about Paula, protectively, his tone more than anything else, as though he cared for her."

"John, she was easy to like. There was something about her."

Wright placed a hand over hers. Then he excused himself and headed toward the men's room, squeezing past the handsome waiter, who was taking orders from two women, a kind of aloof macho about him. The restrooms were three-quarters of the way to the rear, accessible through a short entryway. A woman and the boy who'd had spumoni on his face were emerging from the ladies', and Wright stepped aside, bumping the public phone on the wall, the wall marked with numbers. He scanned them like a bingo player and started to step away. Then his gaze returned to the wall. It took him an extraordinarily long time to comprehend what had caught his eye.

He was in a turmoil and tried not to let it affect his voice as he confronted the proprietor beside a glass counter. The proprietor was carefully loading cannoli into a carton.

"My number's on your wall."

"What?"

"It's written there. My phone number."

"Slow down, friend."

"It's on the wall near the phone."

The proprietor closed the carton and wrapped string around it. "What d'you mean, your number?"

"My number. Come on, I'll show you."

"Easy friend. I don't have to see it. If it's your number, I don't know anything about it. Anybody could've put it there. She could've put it there."

"You said she stopped coming here last fall. She didn't know us then, not till January."

The proprietor knotted the string and snapped it. "So she could've come in here in January without me knowing it. There's all kinds of explanations. Don't work yourself up, and don't cause us both trouble. Neither of us need it."

Wright took a deep breath to get hold of himself. The proprietor picked up the carton and a bag of cookies.

"Here, give these to your wife."

Wright took them because they were thrust against his chest. Merle was standing by the table, waiting for him. Wright spoke briefly to her, and they left. The proprietor motioned to a waiter, the handsome one, and led him to the telephone. He gripped the waiter's upper arm.

"You know where the Lestoil is?"

The waiter nodded.

"Wash every number off that fucking wall."

8

In the glare of late afternoon, Oliver drove his Pinto slowly past the Wrights' house and saw an open garage, no car in sight, no sign of life, which relieved him of an immediate decision. He breathed in the scent of mown grass and accelerated, checking the rearview. When a car approached from the opposite way, he lowered his head as if reaching for something on the seat.

He drove on, in the shade of several varieties of maples, which he considered hearty animals, beautiful beasts in bloom, wild enough to surge and tame enough to root in neighborhoods, a description he'd once shared with students in his Introductory Psych class, his eyes darting to female faces, a few in particular, his favorites. He slowed for a rush of children at play and, getting by them, sped to another street.

Approaching the center of town, he passed East Elementary, where two of his three children were pupils. His oldest, a boy, was in junior high, an honor student. Stopping for lights near the Gulf station, he again checked the rearview, this time for a peek at himself, and his eyes bulged back at him. He was ghostly pale. When a lithe figure passed in front of the

Pinto, a straight-back young woman with generous breasts, he barely glanced at her. When a police cruiser pulled up behind him, he froze, and when the lights changed, the Pinto stalled. When he arrived home, he embraced his wife.

The Wrights returned home in a burnt-orange sunset to the sweetness of cut grass, which instantly unnerved them. Their first thought was that the killer, in a lunatic act of penance, had done the chore. Their second thought was that their daughter was back, her return a sane part of the penance. Wright unlocked the front door and flung it open. In a macabre repeat performance, with every detail of the original sharp in their minds and with the same maddening clumsiness, they mounted the stairs to Marcie's room. Wright banged the door open and then held his wife. The telephone rang seconds later: Mrs. Harrington with the explanation. Merle broke into uncontrollable laughter.

It did not take Wright long to calm her. "I'm sorry," she said. She whipped the hair out of her face and managed a near-normal smile. "I'm all right." She made the coffee.

They took their coffee into the den and sank into chairs. Merle kicked her shoes off and drew her legs up, curling them beneath her. For a moment or so she closed her eyes, exhausted from the day and emotionally drained from the way it ended.

"He meant well," Wright said.

"The chief? I know." She remembered her coffee and sipped it. "What are we going to do about the other thing?"

Wright was quiet.

"I think we ought to tell somebody," she said.

Wright nodded. "But I'd like to wait. I'd like to go back there first and talk to him again. I don't know what good it'll do, but I'd like to try."

"I wish I had seen it too."

"Merle, it was our number. I stared at it long enough. I wasn't mistaken."

"I know you weren't."

"But he could be right. There could be a reasonable explanation."

"But you don't think so."

"I don't know what to think."

"I don't either," she said and laid her head back, her eyes closed again.

Later, as she was undressing in their bedroom, he approached her quietly from behind and touched her bare hips. She swayed against him, and he held her as she stretched an arm back, her fingers blindly finding his face. "John, let's talk about something." Her voice was strange, and he held her tighter. "If we don't ever find Marcie, what's going to happen to us? Will we learn to live with it?"

"Merle, don't ask that."

"You're hurting me."

He eased his grip.

"If not you, John, who else can I ask? Who else would know?"

He moved her around in his arms and kissed her. The room was warm, but she was shivering. He helped her on with her gown.

"Yes," he said. "We'll learn to live with it."

She went to bed, and he stayed up. He set the Sony up on the kitchen table and ate half of a sesame-seed cookie while watching the eleven o'clock news. Later, with his second glass of bourbon, he watched *Police*

Story, an episode with Jackie Cooper as an aging
detective obsessively dedicated to his daughter after
losing his wife, Cooper almost a Chaplin figure in his
pork-pie hat and threadbare suit. The drama distressed Wright as thoroughly as Merle's question had,
but he watched it through. The phone rang during
the concluding commercial.

He caught it on the first ring, an ugly sound he was
sure would wake Merle even though the bedroom phone
did not carry a ring, and he said hello before he got
the receiver to his head. It was that same voice, the
one that produced broken sounds, not words, as if the
speaker were only half human and only half there, the
rest of him stealing away down some street.

"Please," Wright said, directing his eyes to the
ceiling. "Say something I can understand."

The man stopped speaking.

"Don't hang up," Wright pleaded.

But he did.

"You're kidding."

"Would I kid you?"

"Oh, for Christ's sake," the agent with the glasses
said, tipping back in his chair. "Who the hell do they
think they are—Nick and Nora Charles?"

"Well, I can understand their mental state," the stout
agent said. "You know, why they'd do it."

The agent with the glasses rose without a word,
stepping slowly from his desk to the window for a
look down at Boston's mad-hour traffic, which would
determine when he would call it a day. His home was
in Norwood, not an easy drive. His office was on the
ninth floor in the JFK building, with a hazy and clut-

tered view of the North End. Without turning, he asked, "How long were they in there?"

"More than an hour. They were spotted just by chance."

"On the other thing?"

"Right."

"They've got a home. Why don't they stay in it?"

The stout agent wasn't expected to respond and didn't. He glanced at his watch, intending to buck the traffic to his home, which was a worse drive, beginning with the Callahan Tunnel. He smiled. "Want to hear another good one? I was talking to Harty, and he said our friend, Chief Tull, spent the day at the Wrights' house cutting their grass."

The agent with the glasses turned, his face expressionless. "Why?"

"I guess because it needed it. He's a boy scout."

"He's a horse's ass. Any more gems?"

"That's it," said the stout agent with another glance at his watch. He had recently married for a second time and was anxious to get home.

The other agent returned to his chair and made himself comfortable, as if he might stay the evening. He removed his glasses and rubbed his eyes. Carefully fitting the glasses back on, he said, "You made it back in good time. How was Oliver?"

"He wanted to know if he passed."

"A teacher wanting to know if he passed, huh? What did you tell him?"

"I said I didn't know exactly, but there seemed to be some questions."

"Good. How did he take that? Like a man?"

"He took it quietly."

"Too quietly?"

"In a way."

"What's too quietly? Tell me."

"He stared straight ahead looking at nothing. He didn't hear me when I said things."

"Yes, I'd call that quiet," the agent with the glasses said, dropping farther back in his chair. "What about the chip on his shoulder?"

"Too heavy for him. I'd say he knocked it off himself."

"Very good. We still have a tail on him?"

"Yes."

"You look tired. What are you still doing here?"

The stout agent grinned and struggled to his feet. The agent with the glasses waited until he reached the door and had his hand on the knob.

"One last thing before you leave. You've seen where I live, that lawn of mine."

The stout agent nodded.

"Find out how much the chief charges by the hour."

Oliver woke his wife in the dead of night and embraced her. He had surprised her this way once before, only a few nights ago, with an urgency that had frightened her, and this time the urgency seemed greater. She had not questioned his sudden surge of sexual interest in her then and did not now, for she doubted he would tell the truth, and she wasn't sure she wanted the truth, her suspicion being that he was getting over another woman, whose identity she would never want to know. Too much worked against her responding to him, but she positioned herself for his pleasure with her knees pulled back as far as she could manage, as if she were at least a good sport.

He took an ungodly long time.

He fell away from her fast, exhausted, his chest heaving as he fought for breath. His body glistened in the dim light, and she used his discarded T-shirt to sponge the sweat from him. She got a look at his eyes, which seemed awry, ready to blow out.

"You OK?" she asked with alarm.

He nodded from his pillow.

"Can I get you anything?"

He shook his head in a manner almost boyish, as if her concern were all that really mattered. She knew something was clawing him, and she felt it had to be a guilty conscience—that and remorse and an over-whelming need to show his love for her. She wished they could find a way to talk about it.

She was nearly asleep when she felt him move, and opening her eyes she saw the vague sweep of his arm. He was reaching for her. He wanted her again.

"Please," she said, frightened, and resisted.

"From my wife," Chief Tull said. "Homemade coffee cake."

Merle Wright accepted the white bag on its side, heavy because the cake was on a dish, and she thanked him with a forced smile. She let him in, led him to the kitchen and offered him a chair. Wright was not home.

"Where is he?" the chief asked, declining coffee.

"Boston," Merle said, pouring some for herself and joining him at the table. He waited for further explanation and didn't get any. She slipped the coffee cake from the bag. The dish was pink glass, flea-market variety. Her mother had had a set of a slightly darker shade.

"Go ahead, try some," the chief urged. "Her stuff wins prizes at West Parish Church." His face had a shellacked look from a shave and yesterday's sun. He watched her cut two pieces, one larger than the other. "None for me, please, but I want you to try it."

It was good, very good, but she could manage only a bite. She said, "Thank you for cutting our lawn."

He blushed and said, "I didn't finish it all."

She wanted to tell him that she didn't want him doing anything like that again without first letting them know and really she'd prefer he not do it at all. But she didn't want to hurt his feelings, so she said nothing.

"Where were you people yesterday?" he asked in a tone her father might have used with her, and she explained as briefly as possible, mentioning Dorchester and the North End and offering no details. He shook his head vigorously. "You shouldn't go like that on your own. Your husband should know better."

She did not want to argue and remained silent. He pointed a finger at her.

"You never know who you're dealing with, and you don't have badges or guns. You don't have any experience in these things. When's your husband coming home?"

She suddenly felt very tired and in a way defeated. She lifted her coffee cup.

"Mrs. Wright?"

"I'm not sure," she said. "He said he wouldn't be long."

"Tell him to call me as soon as he gets in."

She put the cup down.

"You won't forget?"

"No," she said.

He rose. "You stay there. I'll see myself out."

He took two steps and turned back to look at her. She was staring at him but obviously not seeing him.

"Mrs. Wright, what's the matter?"

"I should've gone with him," she said.

Wright left his car at a private lot near the North Station and made his way into the North End, the morning pleasantly warm and almost unbearably bright, the streets crooked and crowded, everything wedged together: buildings, parked cars and people. The buildings were brick, with potted windowsills, rising six and seven stories to rooftops accommodating grapevines, a private world up there, young black-haired women sunning themselves. According to myth, the neighborhood was the safest in Boston, tourists welcome, but Wright knew enough not to gawk. Women overran the sidewalk at vegetable stalls, and men clustered at corners. Wright edged past a knot of youths trying to look like gangsters. Perhaps they were.

Too early for tourists, the coffee bar had only a scattering of customers, regulars, men Wright's age and older, and only one waiter, the handsome one. The proprietor was sitting at a table far to the rear, and Wright went directly to him. The proprietor looked up without surprise, his lazy eyelid more noticeable than the last time Wright had seen him. Wright sat down without being asked.

"Make yourself at home. How'd you like the cannoli?"

Wright nodded. "It was OK, thank you."

"Too bad I haven't got any more for you. We ran out. How about the cookies?"

"They were good."

"We're out of them too. You understand what I'm telling you?"

Wright did not bother answering. He took out a

cigarette, and the proprietor watched him light it. Both men seemed to relax a little.

The proprietor said, "I'll tell you something now in case you go looking. That wall's been washed. No numbers there anymore."

Wright started to speak and stopped. He waited.

The proprietor said, "You understand why I did it?"

"You don't want any trouble. I don't want to cause you any."

"But you are, friend, just by being here. There are Feds watching this place, do you know what I'm talking about? It doesn't have anything to do with you, only me, but you could make it worse."

"I don't know anything about that. Why are they watching you?"

"I'm a Guinea. They think every Guinea's in the Mafia."

"Are you?"

"Yeah, I've got a machine gun in my pocket."

Wright sat back. Old men were sitting far to his left. He knew they were there by their coughing attacks. He glanced at patrons closer by, men who had looked menacing when he had arrived but now seemed friendly enough, or at least neutral. A solitary man sitting in a corner was handling a deck of cards, giving them a professional shuffle. Wright gradually realized the proprietor was smiling, the smile rather bittersweet.

"You like me, friend?"

"Yes," said Wright. "Yes, I think I do."

The proprietor laughed, regarding him with one eye. "'You have to say that, don't you? You don't even know my fucking name."

"Yes, I do. It's on the sign outside. Feoli."

"OK, you get a cigar, maybe some more cookies. What do I get? Do I have the right to privacy, friend? Or don't I have rights?"

"You've got to understand my position too," Wright said calmly. "That number on the wall, whether it's still there or not, is all I've got right now. And it's got to mean something."

"Nothing. That's what it means."

"But I don't know that."

"You're not calling me a liar, are you?"

"No." Wright tried to keep his voice level. "But maybe something else you know might mean something."

"Friend, don't marry us. It won't work."

Wright glanced away, at the man still shuffling the cards. He listened to distant coughs and saw new arrivals, two tourists. He saw the proprietor look at his watch.

"I don't want to tell you to get out of here, friend, but this place is going to get busy pretty soon. I've got to get ready."

The proprietor rose, and Wright said, "Mr. Feoli, I'm going to look at that wall."

"Christ, you don't even believe me about that. So I don't know what to tell you."

"And I'd like to come back when you have more time, maybe tomorrow."

The proprietor stared hard at Wright, as if to peer into his head. "Friend, don't do it."

Wright had a problem finding his car. He couldn't remember the row, and the sun's glare didn't help. A footstep scrunched behind him, and a voice startled him.

"I think it's over there, Mr. Wright."

Wright turned on one heel and saw the glint of glasses on the long impassive face, which was lifted, as if the sun didn't bother it. Wright and the agent walked toward the Cutlass. "Is this a chance meeting?" Wright asked.

"Not exactly," the agent said, his manner almost military, his presence solemn. He pointed. "You've got a dent there. It looks recent."

"Yes, I know about it."

They stood near the Cutlass. Wright felt the sun settling on his neck and shoulders. The agent said, "I understand you had another crank call. It sounded on tape like the same fellow."

Wright nodded. "I think it was, but he didn't stay on the line very long."

"Yes, we know. Too bad. Maybe next time." The agent glanced away and then returned his eyes slowly. "How was Feoli?"

"Fine," Wright said quickly, to show that the question, other than the cold way it was asked, didn't surprise him. He decided to stay silent for the time being about the business of his telephone number.

"We understand what you're trying to do, Mr. Wright, but why don't you end it?"

"End it?"

"Stay home. We have enough to do without worrying about the safety of you and your wife, and we don't need your help in doing our job."

"You don't understand," Wright said quietly. "You don't understand anything."

The agent's thin nostrils flared. "Let me be frank with you, Mr. Wright. You're blundering into places where you have no business, and you're over your head with Feoli."

"I'm looking for my daughter."

The agent sighed, as if with official regret. "Mr. Wright, we don't think there's much chance your daughter's still alive."

Wright listened to the traffic on nearby Nashua Street. He heard horns. He said, "Show me her body."

"It might never be found."

"Where have you looked?"

"In many more places than you, Mr. Wright."

"I can't promise you anything," Wright said after a hesitation. He reached for the door of the Cutlass. "Can I drop you anywhere?"

The agent turned away without answering.

9

The stout agent phoned Oliver at his home and said, "We'd like you to take another polygraph."

Oliver was silent, as if he had no intention of answering. The agent, though unsettled from a bad night and breakfast he could still taste, was patient. Finally Oliver said, "Why? Why should I? It's not fair."

The agent had had his first fight with his new wife over something silly and had left it unresolved. Losing some patience with Oliver, he said, "I haven't the faintest idea what you mean by *fair*. You came to me for help, and I tried to get you off the hook with a polygraph. The reading, regrettably, was inconclusive. Whose fault is that? Mine? Yours?"

Oliver's voice came through clearly, more manly, a bit sarcastically: "You said we were working with an expert with the very best equipment. What happened?"

"Everybody's fallible, Mr. Oliver. I'm fallible. You're fallible."

Oliver's tone turned unmistakably hostile: "How do I know it was inconclusive? Maybe you people just didn't get the result you wanted, and now you want another chance to hang something on me."

The agent, who had quickly regained his calm, said

smoothly, "I'm sorry you feel that way. And I suppose I could ask you now, 'Is that fair?'"

"Nothing's fair as far as I'm concerned," Oliver said testily. He was in the kitchen, leaning against a large coppertone refrigerator. Stretching the extension cord of the phone, he moved to a window that gave him a partial view of the drive. "And I don't like you calling my house. My wife easily could've been home."

"Easy, Mr. Oliver." The agent's voice was casual. "What we're asking won't take long."

"I know how long it takes. I've been through it. When are you people going to stop bugging me?"

"Foul, Mr. Oliver. I have to holler foul."

Oliver suspected a faint smile behind the voice. He stared out at the sky, blue like a baby blanket.

"Because I don't think we are bugging you." The agent paused. "But I'd like to be very truthful with you, do you mind?"

Oliver's guard went up. "Go ahead."

"We think you have some things bottled up, and that's what's been bothering you. We think you'd really like to let a lot of things out."

Oliver laughed.

The agent's voice hardened. "We think you may know more about Paula Aherne than you've cared to tell us."

Oliver was silent. Then he heaved a sigh, as if to convey relief and immense satisfaction. "I'm glad you've finally laid your cards out because now I can do the same. I'm considering a suit against your office, you in particular. Harassment and invasion of privacy. That's for openers."

The agent did not respond.

"Did you hear me?" Oliver asked in an eruption of confidence, as if he had just won a hand.

"Yes, I heard you," the agent said tonelessly. "That's your own business. Do what you think best. I have other things on my mind, questions, one being why you decided to ride by the Wrights' house. You know when I mean."

Oliver peered down at himself and then out the window. His wife's car, a small Plymouth, entered the drive, back from delivering their two daughters to day camp. Their son had a summer job bagging groceries at Purity Supreme. The sun was silk on the windshield, and he could scarcely see her face, though he clearly saw her hand on the wheel. The car stopped, but she did not immediately get out, her face remaining a glassy grain in the glass. She seemed to be sitting in a hunch, as if she were carrying a burden he knew nothing about. He had a terrible fear that she was staring at him and picking up the agent's voice. He drew back.

"But let's talk about the polygraph," the agent said. "What's your answer?"

He returned to the window and watched his wife climb out of the car. She was wearing a cream-white blouse and a tan skirt, and it struck him forcefully that she was still good-looking, spirited but thoroughly domesticated, which was how he had wanted her, what he demanded.

"What's your answer?" the agent repeated.

Oliver took time to swallow. "I'll let you know," he said, all confidence gone, and hung up.

Two men in a large Chrysler, the waiter behind the wheel and the proprietor in the rear, watched Wright park his car in the lot, and the waiter said, "No wife. He's alone again." They watched him walk from Nashua Street to Causeway, under the shadows of girders and the hammer of elevated trains, and they waited to see whether anyone followed him. No one did.

"I'm glad he's alone," the proprietor said. "The wife makes me nervous."

"She's looks a little Italian, did you notice?"

"She's Italian like I'm Irish."

The Chrysler slid forward, the motor emitting no sound. The waiter had only one finger on the wheel and sat sort of sideways. The proprietor's face was sour and resigned.

"Hold up," he said. "We know where he's going."

The waiter glanced over his shoulder. "But do we know what we're doing."

"Baby-doll. Do me a favor. Shut up."

The driver edged the Chrysler toward the curb, waited awhile, and then let the car drift back into traffic. Wright faded from sight. Ten minutes later the Chrysler, slow-moving, appeared in the heart of the North End, the market area, which seemed impassable. Crowds milled in front of fruit and vegetable stalls, bins of beans and nuts, windows strung with dry salami and sausage. The waiter said, "Well, I think we waited too long. I don't see him."

"That's because you don't look."

Wright was up ahead, to the left, staring at sidewalk racks of cut-rate clothes, mostly dresses. The waiter squinted and said, "Maybe he's going to fool us. Disguise himself in drag."

"And maybe he's waiting for us to catch up."

"Too bad somebody don't grab him and twist his neck."

"You strangle a guy, he's going to shit himself. Always remember that."

Wright had moved on to a fish store, squid on sale, eels on ice, cod laid out in strips. He saw the reflection of the Chrysler, which eased toward him. A window opened, and the proprietor hollered, "Hey, friend, come here!"

The voice startled him, and he stayed where he was, as people shoved by him. Every other youth was styled like John Travolta.

"Come on, nobody's going to bite you." Wright stepped forward, and the proprietor gestured. "Get in."

The crowd seemed to maneuver him that way with hips and elbows. A number of people greeted the proprietor in passing. Wright gave out a short laugh.

"Do you want to take me for a ride?"

"I want to talk to you. Get in, for Christ's sake."

Wright climbed into the rear, as the proprietor moved over. As soon as he shut the door, the window rose, and the car was sealed and slithering through the crowd.

"Did you know we were behind you?" the proprietor asked.

"You'd be surprised how I look over my shoulder now."

The driver slowly negotiated a corner and headed up a street that disconcerted Wright.

"We're not going to your place?"

"No," the proprietor said.

"Then we are going for a ride."

"A little one."

The narrow street was cluttered with cars parked on both sides, half on the sidewalks. Large American models. The driver maneuvered the Chrysler by them in a way Wright felt he never could. He shook his head.

"Why don't the people here buy smaller cars, more practical, I'd think."

The proprietor grinned. "Nobody here buys little. We see a little car, we know a stranger's in the neighborhood. We see a Volkswagen, we vandalize it to make sure it don't come back. That's protecting your property values, isn't that right, Nicholas?"

The driver seemed to nod.

"You know Nicholas, don't you?" the proprietor said. "Say hello to him."

The driver did not turn his head, and Wright did not say hello. The Chrysler meandered out of the North End, back toward the North Station and in the direction of Storrow Drive, one way out of the city.

"Mr. Feoli, where are we going?"

"Don't worry about it. By the way, where's your wife?"

"She's not feeling well. She may come in later, by bus."

"Bus. You only got one car?"

"Yes."

"You poor?"

Wright smiled. "Practical. Maybe a little poor."

The proprietor sighed. "Don't make sense, does it?"

Wright looked down at his hands. "No, it doesn't. It's a nightmare."

The proprietor fell silent, and Wright noticed that they had never reached Storrow Drive but had turned in a different direction. He wasn't sure where they were: Charlestown, perhaps. He saw a reflection of himself in the far window, which was tinted, and he realized for the first time how much he resembled his father, who had died in the prime of life, in the act of tying a shoe. His father had floated dead to the floor with his eyes open, one larger than the other, which hadn't been so in life.

"Friend."

Wright appeared not to hear.

"Friend, I'm the one who wrote your number on the wall."

Wright was still staring at the window but now was seeing nothing, except an advertisement for Salada Tea on some soiled store window. He shivered. The air-conditioning was making him cold.

"But it had nothing at all to do with you or what happened to her. That you've got to understand right away."

"Where are we going?"

"You listening to me?"

"Yes."

"Maybe I could tell you a little more about that girl, but it's nothing that could help you, nothing you need to know, but it could hurt me. You understand?"

"No."

The Chrysler was no longer moving, but the motor seemed to be still running. Wright looked around. They were parked near a demolished building, the wreckage scattered about, bricks made into mountains. The waiter slouched, as if to nap. Wright gave the proprietor a hard look.

"I have a right to know."

"You're not listening."

"I'm listening, but you're not telling me anything."

The proprietor suddenly leaned forward. "Don't waste gas. Shut the fucking motor off."

The waiter did, first lowering the other windows, not the one near Wright.

"His too, for Christ's sake."

The glass vanished, and Wright took a breath. He found his hands trembling and tried to will them to stop. He said, "So far I don't understand anything."

"Let me explain something first," the proprietor said, as Wright searched for cigarettes and lit one with a steady hand. "One reason we're here is because I don't want you coming to my place and sitting there like a fucking sore thumb. It's bad for business, but that's not what worries me. It's what the Feds think."

Wright concentrated on his cigarette, watching the smoke furl out the window.

"You think I don't feel for you, don't you?"

"At this point," Wright said, "I don't know anything, except somebody took my daughter and I want her back. I won't stop until I know what's happened to her. And I have to believe she's alive. I won't believe anything else."

The proprietor moved closer. "Believe me when I tell you this, nobody from my neighborhood had anything to do with it. That's been checked and rechecked, and I'll tell you something else. I don't think anybody from Boston did it either. I could be wrong there, but I don't think so."

Wright opened an ashtray and deposited an ash. A breeze touched his hair.

"Am I getting through to you?" the proprietor asked.

"You know things about Paula Aherne that others don't. I think you should tell me."

The proprietor pulled away and spoke with a weariness: "You think I know a lot, but I don't, and you're making more of it than you should. But I'll make a deal with you. You stay away from my place for a week, and let's see what the Feds come up with. For once I'm on their side. Anyway, we wait a week, and if nothing happens, I'll talk to you again. Deal?"

"A week is a long time."

"Don't bargain. You're getting a gift."

Wright threw away his cigarette. "In a week then, if nothing happens, I go to your place."

The blood rushed to the proprietor's face. "You don't put a foot in my place. I'll get in touch with you." He leaned forward and tapped the waiter's shoulder.

The windows rose silently, and the Chrysler cruised ahead. Wright closed his eyes, as if he were emotionally spent and physically sore. Cool air washed over him, and this time felt good. He was surprised at how fast the Chrysler made it to the lot at the North Station. The proprietor leaned past him and opened the door. Wright hesitated.

"Could you at least tell me if Paula Aherne was her real name?"

"Friend, get out."

Wright was half-way out when the proprietor gripped his arm. The proprietor's left eyelid drooped, but his right eye was clear and cold.

"This conversation, friend. It goes no further."

Wright slid out and felt his legs nearly give when his feet hit the ground. He limped toward his car without looking back. The Chrysler reversed its direction, bounded onto Nashua Street, and made the lights onto Causeway.

"So what's going to happen in a week?" the waiter asked, glancing at the billing on the Pussycat Theater.

"You buy time, even if it ain't worth anything."

"With all due respect," the waiter said, sitting sideways again, "I think you was wrong."

"With all due respect," the proprietor said, "go fuck yourself."

In their sunlit bedroom Oliver undressed his wife and then himself. Her hair, pinned back when she had come home, was now loose. It was dark blond and streaked, at least ten tones in it. In bed he kissed her hair and then her face. He kissed her throat and her shoulders and ran a hand over her body, at times too emphatically. "Please tell me what's bothering you?" she asked, and he murmured, "Nothing, except I love you." He traced a finger over her belly scars from babies, as if they were marks of beauty, her messages of love, signals that she was his forever, which had become urgently important to him. He edged down as she raised a fleshy thigh, a husky leg, and tasted her where she was salty and slightly sour but not in the least unpleasant, his performance swiftly turning more obeisant than sexual. He stayed there too long.

"Please come up," she said. He boosted himself forward and clung to her but did not slide onto her. "Do you want me to get on you?" she whispered, and he shook his head. She reached down and touched him. He was soft.

"I just want to hold you," he said.

Two hours later he was on Route 93 and pushing the Pinto hard, its speed in tune with the violence of his emotions, the speed part of a game. He decided that if a state trooper flagged him down he would take the ticket, turn around and go home. He was not stopped.

He rode a spacious elevator to the ninth floor of the JFK building and entered an office that was not as elaborate and official-looking as he had expected. He asked for the stout agent by name, Mr. Cogger, remembering it only at the last moment.

Agent Cogger viewed him secretly, with a huge feeling of accomplishment and with sharp regret over the timing. He knew he would have to phone his wife sooner or later and tell her not to wait up for him. Deciding to delay the call, he stepped to his desk, picked up the phone, and punched out an interoffice number.

"Guess who's here," he said with a smile in his voice. Then he said, "Yes, that's right. Your office or mine?"

A minute later he escorted Oliver into his office and showed him to a chair. A silver forelock dangled boyishly near Oliver's eyes, which were overly bright, almost stunning. The agent with the glasses entered from a side door, and Cogger, seating himself, said to Oliver, "You remember Mr. Spence, agent in charge."

Oliver rose from his chair with a chunky cough and a semihysterical smile. "It's ironic," he said, clearing his throat with a painful sound. "I knew her, but I never got anywhere with her. Can you believe that?"

10

He rumpled his hair back and talked without inter-
ruption except for those times when he spoke too fast
and Agent Spence quietly told him to slow down and
another time when Agent Cogger replaced the cart-
ridge in the tape recorder. He talked until his throat
went dry and he had to ask for water. He watched
Spence remove his glasses to polish them with a special
tissue, and for the first time the agent appeared human
to him, a man naked under his clothes like anyone
else and with eyes for the moment weak and vulnerable,
which gave Oliver hope. He waited for questions, but
they wanted him to continue talking. The questions
came much later, hard and fast, and this time his throat
went dry in midsentences. At one point he croaked,
"Do you think I killed her? I didn't. I only knew her."
He hung his head. "I did what I could for her. I tried
to help her."

"Look at us," Spence said in the tone of an officer
bringing an enlisted man to attention, and Oliver
brought his head up abjectly, no longer sure of the
other's humanity. "Did you ever make anonymous calls
to the Wrights?"

"I swear to God I didn't."

The questioning intensified, and he lost track of time and then the ability to give answers. "Please," he said and asked for more water. Both agents looked at their watches. Spence gave him permission to call his wife, but he declined.

"Does she know you're here?" Spence asked.

"No."

"Then you should call her," said Cogger, who earlier had had an abrupt and unsatisfactory conversation with his own wife.

Oliver remained silent. Then he asked to use the bathroom, and Cogger directed him to it. Afterward Cogger took him to a small conference room and left him there alone. He stared at blank walls and the closed door. The room was windowless and seemingly sealed, but he felt drafts and imagined himself exposed, as if he were treading deep water in the presence of unseen fish, for he was sure he was being watched, which was how he'd felt while standing at the urinal. He took a seat at the conference table and started to shiver.

A half hour later the door popped open, and Cogger appeared with his hands full and with a legal-sized yellow pad tucked under an arm. "Sorry I took so long," the agent said, surprising Oliver with a thick ham-and-cheese sandwich, which Oliver would not touch, but he grabbed the coffee that came with it, spilling some. Cogger quickly supplied napkins.

"I don't know why I'm shivering," Oliver said, managing a laugh.

"No reason to," Cogger said. "It's quite warm in here."

"I suppose you think only the guilty shiver," Oliver said with another laugh. He wanted Cogger to sit down so that he could talk with him, but Cogger remained standing and then suddenly dropped the yellow pad on the table, along with a pen.

"No rush on this," Cogger said casually, "but when you're up to it, Mr. Spence would like you to write down everything you've told us so far."

"I've told you everything," Oliver said, his face stricken. "I swear it. And you've got it all on tape."

"You may have forgotten a few details. Take your time."

Oliver was alone again, treading water. His hand shook as he wrote, and he could scarcely read his own handwriting. He made several false starts, tearing the discarded sheets into little pieces. He had trouble remembering dates and places and was in dread of contradicting himself. When he finally finished, he fell back exhausted. Moments later an agent he had never seen before entered and took away his four-page statement, parts of which were illegible. Then Cogger reappeared.

"You're tired, aren't you, Mr. Oliver?"

"Yes. Yes, I am."

"Mr. Oliver, what did you do with the Wrights' baby?"

"Oh, my God," he said, and for an instant or so it seemed he would faint.

A folding cot with a pillow and a gray blanket was set up for him in a distant office. He did not want to lie down, but they insisted—Cogger and other agents, Spence was not there. He closed his eyes, and when he opened them he knew he had slept because he had dreamed he was on the verge of a forest, ready to run into it, and because he had an urgent need to use the bathroom. An agent, appearing at the door, anticipated his need, escorted him down the hall, and opened the door for him. Cogger was at one of the sinks, cleaning his jaws with a battery-shaver. He smiled at Oliver in the mirror and said, "What would you like for breakfast?"

"I'd like to have it at home," Oliver said, removing himself to a distant urinal.

Cogger clicked off the shaver. "I'm afraid not, sir."

Oliver closed his eyes. "I'm not hungry."

At MIT, with a tube wrapped around his chest, a clamp on his arm and electrodes poised against his skin, the polygraph measured his breathing, his blood pressure and his sweating. "Just relax," the bearded man said, but Oliver couldn't. His heart throbbed, and he sweated a lot.

"Are you wearing a wrist watch?"

"Yes."

"Do you carry an American Express card?"

"Yes."

"Is your wife's name Barbara?"

"Yes."

"Did you ever hit anybody with a hammer?"

"God, no," he said and began to cry.

Spence's office was larger than Cogger's, and Spence sat with a flag behind his desk and Jimmy Carter's picture on the wall, no others. "Let's go over it again," he said to Oliver, who lowered his head as if in pain. "I like to see a man's eyes," Spence said brusquely, and Oliver looked up, bedraggled, in need of a shave. "We're alone, Mr. Oliver. No tape recorder, nothing. No pressures."

"I still haven't been told how I did this time," Oliver said in the tone of a student asking about grades.

"Not well."

"Inconclusive?"

"Unsatisfactory." Spence reached for sheets of paper on his desk, Oliver's handwritten statement. "I had trouble reading this. That's partly why I want you to go over it again."

Oliver's hands slipped from his lap. "I met her where I told you."

"Tell me again."

"Holly's. A disco bar near Boston University. I thought she was a student, except, as I said before, she seemed different, as if she wasn't part of that scene but just peeking in, not looking for any . . . any company."

"Then why did you bother with her? You were there for obvious reasons."

"I don't know."

"Sure you do. What was she, a challenge?"

"I don't know."

"Keep your eyes up, Mr. Oliver, your voice too." Spence rattled Oliver's papers, glancing at the top one, then discarding it with a grimace. "I find that interesting. She didn't want company, but she accepted yours."

"Because she *was* looking for something," Oliver said, sitting rigidly, as if he could see her ghost. "She thought the place had a college atmosphere just because college kids were there, and that's what we talked about, how she'd like to get into BU or any college but couldn't because of her high school grades. She said she'd been sick a lot."

"So you offered to help."

"Yes."

"Did you by chance get her drunk?"

"I swear I didn't. All she had was beer, and she never finished what was in her glass."

"What were you drinking?"

"Scotch and water. It was weak Scotch, very weak."

"How many weak Scotches did you have, Mr. Oliver?"

"I don't remember. Maybe three at the most."

Spence put his hands flat together, matching the fingers, and raised them to his chin. "All right, Mr. Oliver, and then you drove her home."

Oliver shook his head hard. "No, I didn't drive her home, and I told you I didn't. She wouldn't let me. She said she had a strict aunt who watched out the window."

"Oh, yes." Spence sighed, as if bored. "Let's move ahead. By the way, are we firm on the date of this?"

"Yes. During the semester break, January third, Tuesday, I'm sure of it."

"Pretty cold night."

"No, it was warmish, considering."

"You remember that?"

"Yes."

"Fine, let's skip to the next day. By arrangement you came back to Boston, picked her up at the North Station, and then drove back to Ballardville with her."

"Yes," said Oliver, his voice stale. He looked headachy. "I showed her the town and the college, and because she was so far behind academically I suggested she might just want to monitor classes for a semester, to get her feet wet. I gave her a list of courses, large enrollments, where she wasn't likely to be noticed."

"Including one of your own courses."

"Yes."

"You certainly went out of your way for her, Mr. Oliver. Had you done this for others?"

"No."

"Then why'd you do it for her?"

Oliver squared his shoulders. "I wanted us to be friends."

"Speak plainly. You wanted her for sex."

"Yes," Oliver said and lowered his eyes. Spence allowed it. Spence, still with his fingers perched at his chin, rested his own eyes. He even seemed to catch a moment's nap. He dropped his hands.

"All right, Mr. Oliver. Then you were on your way back to Boston with her. Take it from there."

"I pulled over at a rest area." Oliver's voice was weak, and he forced himself to raise it. "I was very attracted to her, and then I guess I was a little rough. She wouldn't lie flat."

"What did she do?"

"She jumped out of the car. She ran."

"What did you do? Mr. Oliver, I think you'd better look at me. Makes it easier to hear."

"I drove back to Ballardville."

"And how did she get back to Boston?"

"I don't know," Oliver said miserably and looked toward a wall. "I never expected to see her again, but two weeks later when the semester started she showed up in my class, sat way in back. I almost didn't recognize her. She'd cut her hair like a boy's."

"And what did you do?"

"Nothing. I ignored her."

Spence sat back. "Everytime she came to your class you ignored her. Why?"

"I don't know." Oliver's voice became nasal. "I guess I thought she might be trouble."

"Did she ever try to talk to you?"

"No, never."

"Did you know she was babysitting for the Wrights?"

"No, not till all of this happened."

"Why didn't you tell us this story then?"

Oliver reached for a handkerchief. "I was afraid," he said and flinched as Spence stared at him intensely with a lipless smile. "What's the matter?"

"I'm a little fascinated by you, Mr. Oliver. By the way, you can speak to your wife if you like. She's waiting in Agent Cogger's office."

"Who called her?"

"We did."

Oliver started to rise and didn't make it on the first try. He was holding his handkerchief and appeared physically wounded. Spence still had the thin smile.

"Do you consider me an intelligent person, Mr. Oliver?"

"Yes."

"Then why are you blowing smoke up my ass?"

"What's he doing?" Spence asked.

"Crying on his wife's titty," Cogger said. "You know, we could hold him forever on an obstruction charge."

"I don't want to hold him."

Cogger looked surprised, and then tried not to show it. He waited, watching Spence tip back in his chair. He tried to read the long laconic face.

Spence said, "What's your impression of Chief Tull?"

Cogger smiled.

Spence said, "What do you think would happen if somebody, unbeknownst to us, put a bug in the chief's ear about Mr. Oliver."

Cogger laughed.

Spence sat forward. "Let's do it."

Cogger left Spence's office, but within five minutes he was back, more than a little bemused. "Excuse me," he said, more forcefully than usual. "I just learned the Wrights got another one of those phone calls. This time the wife took it."

"Same fellow?"

"Yes, except this time, after making those noises, he said something." Cogger paused, as if for breath.

"Don't be dramatic. What'd he say?"

"He said 'I didn't do it.' Then hung up."

"Was it traced?"

"No."

Spence's face was blank, Cogger's flushed. Spence shrugged.

"Sir," Cogger said. "Oliver couldn't have made the call."

Spence tipped back. "That doesn't change anything." Cogger started to leave, and Spence said, "Just a minute. I've been thinking. I'd like those things installed."

Cogger showed surprise. "That could be difficult."

Spence sighed. "That's not even worth a response, is it?"

11

The sun glared, and the man inside the glass phone booth appeared encased in ice. When he stepped out he stumbled and for too many moments stared at the sidewalk, as if the fault were there and not in himself. He walked stiffly into the Boston Common, disturbing pigeons as he followed an asphalt path to a bench, one of the few vacant. Sitting with his legs crossed, he appeared peaceful and a little tired when in fact he was giddy. He watched a squirrel high in a tree, a small gray ghost floating from one branch to another, flying without wings. His head tilted, he peered at people from an angle and saw all the women who passed, none of the men. When a slim young woman in denim shorts, flower designs embroidered on the hips, stopped to adjust a sandal, he glanced quickly away. He sat for nearly an hour before making a half-decision.

He cut across the Common, walking briskly over the grass, steering clear of people lying on it, including a derelict whose body was tightly curled, as if hibernating. He hiked to a phone booth, a different one from before, this one near the Public Gardens and in the shade. He sealed himself in the glass cubicle and stared at the phone as if it were a queer prize. He ran a hand into his hair, which looked electrically charged. The lines in his forehead were taut. Slowly he took coins from his pocket, the right amount, and deposited a dime, with the rest ready. He hoped the woman would answer again. He knew the number as if it were his own and began punching the digits solidly, but reaching the last digit he punched a two instead of a one and abruptly racked the phone, his hand shaking so badly he shoved it into a pocket. For a second he thought he might be sick. He pushed open the cubicle and freed himself as if from a grave.

The day was moist and cloying, and he loosened his tie. He looked like a manual laborer who had been given a suit of clothes for a special occasion, the suit old-fashioned and improperly pressed. He walked rapidly, his body alternately hot and cold, to a distant parking lot, where he destroyed the stringed receipt wedged beneath the left wiper on his car. The car was nine years old and took time starting.

He drove west out of Boston on Route 2. He maintained a steady fifty miles an hour. Had he driven faster, the car would have vibrated. The ride, smooth at first, became rough. He was hitting creases in the road, which did him and his car little good. He felt each jounce throughout his body, like punishment, and watched the green along the highway give way to land that had been pulled apart. Boulders hung threateningly out of banks of gravel, and some had tumbled into gullies. He did not relax until some time later when the road rose as if to the sky, cresting, flattening out, giving him a view of green hills that looked furry. He was near home.

Home was a tiny city of old brick factories and

wooden ones painted red, an immigrant community that had once accommodated a furniture industry and an overcrowded downtown. The furniture factories were now mostly abandoned, and many stores were razed or boarded up. His house was a saltbox in need of painting and overwhelmed by an old oak alive only on one side. Its roots buckled the tiny lawn, and dead branches hung over the roof like giant cobwebs.

His wife, who had just got home herself, greeted him with what was nearly a smile and would have been a real one had she thought he would return it. "How was the game?" she asked, even though she knew the Red Sox hadn't played that day, for she had checked the paper, and had they played he would've needed to leave by the fifth inning or so to be home by now.

"Good," he said and climbed the stairs to the bathroom.

"Are you hungry?" she hollered from the stairbottom.

"No," he said and flushed to hide his sound.

She prepared supper anyway, still in her soiled white uniform. She was a nurse's aide at the Gardner hospital, which accounted for most of their income. He had not worked fulltime since he was fired three years ago from one of the remaining furniture factories. He came down the stairs and said, "I told you I wasn't hungry." But he sat down and waited to be served.

Later, when she went down to the basement to do a wash, he climbed the stairs again and went to a room that had not been occupied for six years. The small bed was stripped to the mattress and dust coated the mahogany surface of a child's desk he had made himself, very intricate work, lovingly done. The desk was worth at least three hundred dollars and possibly much more, but he knew he would never part with it. He went to a bureau, opened the bottom drawer, and carefully removed a photograph album, Woolworth variety, an old one that was falling apart. He had started it when the child was six, when he and his wife had got her. He rested the album on the bare top of the bureau and slowly peeled pages. Color Kodaks of the girl when her hair was a white-blond tangle of curls, and some of him when his hair was as black as printer's ink. His wife was fair, so the child had seemed naturally theirs, or at least hers. A closeup of the child displaying a leaf wih insect eggs etched on the underside: tiny perfect dots of silver, like icy sprinkles on a cupcake. Several shots of her playing under the oak, her favorite place, and one showing her blowing out candles on her eighth birthday. Again when she was nine. Ten. A picture of her at eleven, her curly hair grown long, her legs sturdy and suntanned. No pictures of her when she was twelve, and none when she was thirteen.

"You ought to throw that away."

His wife's voice, and immediately his shoulders straightened, and his hands fell from the album. He did not turn around, angry that she had caught him in the room. He could feel her eyes on his back.

"You only hurt yourself looking at it," she said in a voice that sounded accusatory. He turned slowly and glared at her. "What am I supposed to do, keep my mouth shut forever?" she asked, coming close to saying something on her mind for six years. His face filled with blood. He closed the album, returned it to its place, and headed toward the doorway. Had she not moved, he'd have knocked her aside.

Later, in the living room, she wanted to tell him about her day at the hospital, but he pretended to be engrossed with the television. She went to the bathroom, locked herself in, and ran tub water. While undressing, she viewed herself in the mirror, her fleshy face ballooning back at her. Her hair was now gray, and she had never had eyebrows unless she colored them in, but as a young woman she had been pretty and her husband jealous, enough so that she had once cut her hair to make herself less attractive. She lowered herself into the tub and soaked in it until the water went cold.

She set the alarm, turned out the light, and crawled into bed. Her husband lay on his side with the covers almost over his head. She lay flat on her back, her hands clasped under her breasts, knowing he would not touch her even if they were to lie wide-awake all night. She thought of the child, who had run away at thirteen, and she wished bitterly she had had a child of her own, a boy. An hour later, she was still awake, and she knew he was. She said, "Walter, what's the matter?"

He didn't answer.

"I know you're awake," she said.

"Nothing's the matter," he said.

"Stay home tomorrow."

"Why?" he asked, his voice gruff.

"You might do something foolish," she said and began to cry.

Chief Tull took a coffee break in the luncheonette in Ballardville's center. He was sitting at a window table with half a cruller in his mouth when he saw John Wright parking his car across the street. He chewed rapidly and swallowed hard, wiped the sugar from his chin, and reached the car before Wright got out. "Stay there," he said and climbed in from the other side. "You were supposed to call me three days ago. I left word with your wife. Didn't she tell you?"

"Yes, I'm sorry. I meant to." Wright's voice was low. "She hasn't been feeling well."

"How is she now?"

"Better."

The chief squinted. "I suppose you've been back to Boston anyway?"

Wright didn't answer.

"You're fooling yourself," the chief said almost angrily. "The answers are in this town, not off somewhere."

"Then give me some answers."

Instead the chief gave him a self-assured smile. "You think I've been sitting on my butt, don't you? Instead of answers, let me ask you a question. What do you know about this guy Oliver works with you at the college?"

"Paula Aherne was monitoring one of his courses."

"Yeah, but what do you know about him?"

Wright became agitated. "What do you mean?"

"I don't mean anything. I'm only asking." The chief smiled, and Wright felt the sudden pressure of the chief's thumb against his arm. "He likes the girls, could I be right on that?"

Wright let out his breath. "That's no secret, Chief, but I don't think Paula would've given him the time of day, and if she had I'd have heard about it."

The chief was still smiling but smugly now. "I've got ways of getting information, and sometimes it just comes to me, nature of the game, Mr. Wright. What if I was to tell you the FBI regard him as a prime suspect, but can't get anything out of him? He teaches psychology, right? Well, he's psyched them out, in fact made God-damned fools of them."

"Chief," Wright said slowly. "I don't think he's got a bone in his body. I think he's harmless."

"Nobody's harmless," the chief said, drawing back, the blotches on his face swelling, as if Wright had bruised him. "I've read books on Charles Starkweather, Richard Speck and Albert DeSalvo. You could've called them harmless too. Let me tell you something, mister. People are capable of doing anything, no matter how dumb, filthy, crippled, or insane it might be. I'm a policeman, and that's how I know."

Wright was silent. Then again he felt the pressure of the chief's thumb.

"I didn't mean to come on so strong, Mr. Wright. Sorry."

Wright stared at stores, as if trying to remember why he had come downtown. He had an elbow out the window and felt rain in the air. He saw a few dark drops on the sidewalk, like spent coins. He said, "What are you going to do?"

"Check him out." The chief's smile was back. "In my own way."

"You'll let me know right away if you come up with anything?"

"Guaranteed."

Wright left a bag of groceries on the kitchen table and went into the den, where Merle was sitting on the edge of the couch and the two agents were rising from their chairs. Spence's manner was more remote than ever. His face looked dried out, and his mouth was sealed. Cogger spoke.

"We were just leaving."

"No calls?" Wright asked.

"No," said Cogger, "but we've given your wife instructions."

Wright looked at Merle, who tried to smile and failed. Her hair was drawn back, and she was extremely pale. He said to Cogger, "I think the last call was significant. It's the first time he's called during the day, and it's the first he's spoken."

"We realize that," said Cogger. "The telephone company's working very closely with us on this."

Spence, almost without moving his mouth, said, "We may have heard the last of him."

Wright threw him a sharp look. "Why do you say that?"

"It's only a guess, Mr. Wright, but I think he said all he's going to. He proclaimed his innocence to your wife, and it took him this long to do it. Quite an effort."

"Why did he bother?"

Spence almost smiled. "Have you read Kafka? That's one explanation."

"I've read Kafka, but maybe he hasn't."

Spence consulted his watch. "He could be anybody, Mr. Wright. He could be carrying that sketch of Paula Aherne in his pocket and the guilt of the world on his shoulders. If this were New York, I'd say he was a *Daily News* reader."

"This is Ballardville."

Spence gave Cogger a nod.

The agents left, and Wright joined Merle on the couch. They sat together holding hands, not speaking, listening to thunder and glimpsing lightning. The rain came suddenly, thrashing the windows, as if to scratch the glass and crack the panes. Wright squeezed Merle's hand, for they were remembering the same thing about their daughter. Thunderstorms had never scared Marcie, only bewildered her, like toys that were too big.

Merle said, "He's wrong, you know."

"Who?"

"The agent. He's wrong about the man. The man was no stranger to Paula. There was too much feeling in his voice."

Wright put his arms around her, and they lay back together and waited for the phone to ring.

Oliver lay with his wife, who said, "This won't solve anything." He nuzzled against her and then pressed hard, as if he could not get close enough. She pushed the forelock from his face and said, "Listen to me, we've got to talk."

"I've told you everything," he said, his voice child-like. He touched her where she was sore, and he said, "I'm sorry." Shifting his hand to her legs, he lifted one. She had a few broken blood vessels on the inside of her calf. Tracing a finger over them, he said, "I love these."

"I don't." She kicked her leg free and dropped it. "This is becoming foolish. We're going to get bed sores."

"Do you love me?" he asked.

"I don't know anymore," she said. "We've got to talk some more."

Instead he embraced her.

The house was bugged: kitchen, family room, and master bedroom. The listening devices were sensitive enough to pick up a sigh. The receiver was in a telephone company van parked on the street two houses away. A car pulled up behind the van, and two men got out: Spence and Cogger. When they climbed into the back of the van, the agent working the receiver smiled at them. He had on the clothes of a telephone worker. Spence squatted down and said, "What are they doing now?"

The agent, still smiling, shook his head. "You won't believe this, but they're screwing again."

"Turn it up," said Cogger.

"You know me?"

Oliver froze. He had just stepped into the garage and was about to open the door of the Pinto when the voice came at him. From the corner of his eye he saw a face glazed with sweat, a tall figure of a man who suddenly whipped open his poplin jacket to reveal his badge. Oliver knew Chief Tull by sight and nodded.

"You know what I want?" the chief asked. His voice was thick. Oliver was slow to answer. "I asked you a question."

"I'm not sure."

"Keep your voice down. Your family home?"

Oliver nodded.

"I've got questions. Mine you're going to answer. Is that clear?"

Oliver stood riveted, his shoulders trembling. "Yes," he said in a near-whisper, staring at the bright sweat on the chief's nose.

"Paula Aherne. That name means something to you, doesn't it?"

Oliver forced himself to nod.

"You ever stand across the street from where she lived?"

"No, I swear to God I didn't."

The chief made a fist and struck Oliver in the fore-head, the sound like a mallet hitting a wooden block, the blow forceful enough to knock Oliver down. "On your feet!" the chief said, growing hysterical.

Oliver could not or would not move. He lay silently on his back on the concrete floor, though his face appeared active, clamorous, as if he were screaming. The chief unholstered his weapon, the Magnum, which was clumsy in his hand. He almost dropped it.

"You suckered the FBI, but you're not going to sucker me!"

He bent over Oliver and placed the enormous barrel of the Magnum at Oliver's forehead, which was rapidly swelling, the skin torn and scattered.

"The truth! Give it to me!"

Oliver fainted.

The chief gagged and straightened fast, for Oliver's bowels had let loose. He looked down at Oliver with horror. The welt on the forehead looked like a hole, and he wondered whether he had pulled the trigger and somehow failed to hear the explosion. He shoved the Magnum into his holster and heard his stomach gurgle.

Quickly and quietly, he left the garage, not absolutely certain Oliver was alive.

12

She came home in her stained white uniform and heard the crisp fiery noise of paper slippers, one of many pairs she had pilfered for him. He was in the kitchen, shuffling from the stove to the table with coffee he had just poured into a mug. She knew he had not left the house because he was unshaved and wearing work pants that were baggy and low-slung, the fly half unzipped. Sitting at the table, he spooned three lumps of sugar into the coffee and stirred hard. He did not acknowledge her presence until she spoke.

"Thank you," she said.

"For what?"

"For staying home," she said and watched his face darken. She had known that would anger him, but she had felt compelled to say it. She joined him at the table. The photograph album was on the table, spread open. She had seen it immediately but chose to ignore it, though her urge was to close it, for it lay as a flaunt, perhaps a challenge, which she felt unfair, for there was nothing to challenge, unless it was himself. The album was open to the final page of pictures, when the child was eleven, a tightly furled flower ready to blossom into beauty.

"I brought you something," she said and lay near him a wrapped cube of chocolate peppermint, which she had taken from a patient's tray. He looked away, even though the candy was a favorite. She said, "I did a lot of thinking today."

"I don't want to hear," he said. His eyes were on the album, on a picture of himself, prominently displayed, his wiry hair black, his face lit with a smile. Then suddenly he sat back, his lips pushed outward and his face sour.

"I'd like to move," she said. "We could go to Florida. We always used to talk about that."

He sipped his coffee. He had nothing to say.

"Plenty of hospital work for me down there," she said. "I could even work in a rest home. I'm good with old people." That morning she had watched an old man die, with no family near him and maybe none anywhere. He had arched his back, gasping, trying to say something, and she had held his hand instead of calling a nurse.

"Walter," she said.

"What?"

"Will you think about it?"

He got up from the table and left.

She picked up the candy, saving it for him. She took the album and climbed the stairs, her face flushing pink from the strain. She replaced the album in the room that had been the child's, Patricia's, which was an oven, the windows closed, the sun pouring through the glass. Patricia was gone, but shreds remained: a couple of done-up dresses in the closet; a number of school papers, all with *A*'s and *B*'s, preserved in the bureau drawer. She would have preferred destroying the traces and ridding the room of the ghost, but her husband would not have it.

After supper they spent the evening as usual. He watched television, and she took her long bath, as if the tub were her bed, for at times she seemed asleep. At other times she moved her body in certain ways, as if it were capable of sucking up all the water. She thought of the old man who had died that morning, his flimsy white hair and morsel of a mouth, his features knotting instead of relaxing when the moment came, her hand locked in his, as if he were trying to take her with him. She wondered what it would have been like to go with him, whether they would have stayed together.

She wound the alarm, turned off the light, and got into bed, sitting instead of lying. Her husband was buried under the covers. Determined that something had to be settled, she said, "Walter, listen to me for a minute. What may have happened in this house should always stay in this house. Do you agree?"

He pretended to be asleep.

"Walter!" she shouted. "Do you agree?"

He didn't answer, or if he did she didn't hear him. She slid down and lay on her back, knees raised as if she were back in the tub.

She slept badly and rose before the alarm went off. Before leaving for the hospital, she destroyed the album and left the remains for him to see, along with the chunk of candy she had saved.

Cogger, entering Spence's office, said, "I think Chief Tull scared himself more than he did Oliver. He hasn't left the station since it happened. I wished we'd had a microphone in the garage."

"I don't care about the chief," Spence said. "What's Oliver doing?"

"Nothing. He's not sticking his nose out either, and

he's keeping his mouth shut. He told his wife he fell. That's what our guy picked up."

"You're saying he's not scared?"

"No, I think he's plenty scared, but so far he's not doing what we want."

"Then maybe we ought to hold our arms out," said Spence. "Let him know it's easier to deal with us than a crazy chief, since he didn't seem to get the message. Let him know who his friends are."

Cogger looked worried. "I think first we ought to get that van off the streets. Kids are starting to play around it. And we ought to get those microphones out as soon as possible."

"Everything stays until I tell you otherwise," Spence said sharply. "What about that singles' place, Holly's? Did we come up with anything there?"

"No," said Cogger with a sigh. "What makes it bad is the crowd changes practically every night. Christ, there're a hundred Olivers there all looking for the same thing and getting it."

"Meaning there are a hundred Paula Ahernes?"

"Just about."

"Did you check this out personally?"

"Yes."

"OK," Spence said in a voice of dismissal and tipped back in his chair. Cogger lingered.

"Sir, I was wondering if I might take a little vacation time next week. The wife and I—"

Spence snapped forward. "Are you out of your mind?"

The proprietor and the handsome waiter sat at the table near the espresso machine. Women at a nearby table eyed the waiter as he pushed a stick of sugarless gum into his mouth. He was dressed in street clothes, in a fancy suit and an open silk shirt with a spread collar. His sunglasses were wraparound, a mask. He looked like a Hollywood star on a trip home, the proprietor like his immigrant uncle.

The proprietor said, "I've been thinking it over, and maybe you're right. I shouldn't tell that guy nothing."

The waiter chewed slowly, smiling at the women. "Well, it surprised me. It wasn't like you, you know?"

"That kid meant a lot to me."

"But it's like you say yourself," the waiter said. "You've got to keep things in perspective."

"She was like family," the proprietor said, his voice distant. "I thought of her as a niece. That's maybe hard for you to understand."

"No, I understand," the waiter said, "but you don't owe the guy nothing."

"No, I don't, but that don't mean I wouldn't help him if I could."

"Right," the waiter said. "If it didn't mean that maybe you might get hurt."

"What I would like to do is get the guy who did this thing."

"We tried."

"I know."

"Nobody knows nothing."

"I know, I know."

The proprietor drummed his fingers on the table, and the waiter glanced back at the women, all of whom were in culottes. One had oyster-white hair and a leathery tan and was giving him a small smile as she wiped a pastry flake from the edge of her mouth. The waiter's smile was stolen straight from a popular wine commercial on television.

"That don't mean I want us to stop trying," the proprietor said. The waiter was slow to respond, and the proprietor said, "Look at me when I talk. Forget you're a fucking tourist attraction."

"The word's still out, you know that."

"Yeah, but that's all I know," the proprietor said, bending over his coffee, which he hadn't touched and probably wouldn't. The waiter, though still attentive to the women, was watchful of everyone who entered, and with no change of expression he said quietly, "You've got trouble."

Without moving his head, only one eye, the proprietor peered toward the door and muttered, "Sonofabitch, I told him I didn't want him near here."

"And the week's not up," the waiter said from the side of his mouth. "You want me to get him out?"

"No," said the proprietor, with a scowl at the table of women. "Go give your fans a thrill. Tell them you own the joint and is everything all right."

The waiter slipped away, and the proprietor sat back, his left eyelid flickering. Wright's approach was slow, and the proprietor's smile was quick. He flung out a hand. "Sit down, friend. You like pasta?"

The table was small, and their knees nearly bumped. "I'm not hungry," Wright said.

"Just as well. We don't serve it. How about something to drink?"

"You probably don't serve that either."

"You're right. A lot of things we don't serve here, including people who've been told to stay away, and I think that means you, friend."

"I'm sorry," Wright said, "but I couldn't wait." He was about to say more, but an elderly waiter came to the table. "No thank you," Wright said. "I don't want anything."

"Yes, he does," said the proprietor. "Get him a cannoli. Wrap it up. He's going to take it with him."

The old waiter departed smartly, and Wright, narrowing his eyes, said, "I'm not leaving yet. You know things about Paula Aherne. You said you were going to tell me."

"Did I?"

"You said you knew who she was."

The proprietor pointed a fast finger. "Don't put shit in my mouth, friend. I'm not going to eat it."

"What did you say then?"

A passing customer glanced down at them, and the proprietor looked away, more angry at himself than at Wright. His breathing was heavy, as if hurting him. The waiter put a small white bag on the table, near Wright.

"That's your cannoli," the proprietor said. "Take it."

"Later."

"Take it now," the proprietor said, holding back his temper. "Neither of us are going to do any more talking here. Walk out of here, turn left, and keep going. You come to different streets, keep bearing left. If there are no Feds on my ass, I'll pick you up. Otherwise, goodby."

"I'll come back."

The proprietor reddened. Then he steadied himself. "Go on, get out of here. Take the bag."

Wright walked slowly through the sidewalk crowd, the sun burning into his clothes. He passed an old man whose cigar breath was detectable six feet away and sidestepped dog dung, a woman in black, children rushing by him. Buildings broke suddenly into alleyways, as if they were openings into places that on other days might not be there. He nearly ventured into one, backing off when he saw two men mumbling to each other. He lost track of time, took too many lefts, and found himself on Commercial Street, in sight of the Charlestown Bridge. With all cadence gone from his step, he began to backtrack. The Chrysler came upon him from nowhere.

"Get in!"

Wright climbed into the front passenger side and said, "Just you and me?"

"Just you and me," the proprietor said and accelerated. When they made their first turn Wright knew where they were going, and when they cruised over the bridge, striking metal plates that sounded as if they might fly up, he glanced down at the harbor, a peaceful scene. A number of small boats, some with sails, shimmered on the water, and Wright wondered why photographers and painters usually went to the banks of the Charles and seldom here. The proprietor unfurled a handkerchief and blew his nose loudly.

The proprietor parked near a mountain of rubble, near where the waiter had parked, which to Wright seemed months ago. It was not yet midsummer, and Wright felt it had been summer forever. A stray cat appeared near the rubble, poked about, and then disappeared.

"I used to have a cat," the proprietor said, relaxing behind the wheel, scratching an arm. "I called it Rasputin because I once tried to kill it and couldn't. I even threw it against a wall. What d'you think of that?"

"I don't think the story's true," Wright said. "I think you told it to show me you know who Rasputin was and you're capable of violence. It's funny, Mr. Feoli, but you don't scare me, maybe a mistake on my part."

The proprietor looked slowly at Wright. "A big mistake, friend. People who are scared usually stay alive. When I was your age I didn't go nowhere without a shotgun and a forty-five in the trunk of my car. And I always had something handy in the glove compartment."

"If you'll tell me about Paula Aherne, I won't bother you anymore."

"Friend, this is going to pain you, but I don't know nothing about her. I was giving you a line to get you off my back for a while."

Wright shook his head. "No, you weren't."

"Friend, you're calling me a liar. You accept what I say, you understand, because you got no choice. And I don't ever want you coming near my fucking place again, and right now I want you out of my car. You can walk back to yours."

Wright did not move, and the proprietor stared at him with one eye closed, the other gigantically open.

"Guys have been dumped here, you know what I mean? So come on, get the fuck out!"

Wright banged against the door. The proprietor had struck him on the upper arm, a fast brutal jab from a fist, the pain shooting into Wright's shoulder.

"You going to get out?"

"No."

Wright rubbed his arm, which was going numb. The pain stayed in the shoulder. The proprietor opened his fist and looked at his hand. He kept his gaze there and said, "I don't understand you, friend. I really don't."

"It's quite easy. My wife and I can't go on the way we are."

The proprietor was silent for a long while, looking out the window. When he finally looked back at Wright, his face was softer and his voice subdued. "Where's that cannoli?"

"In my suitcoat pocket."

"You going to eat it?"

"No."

"Give it here."

"I can't move my arm."

The proprietor leaned toward him and freed the bag. He looked into it and said, "It's crushed." He ate a chunk of the cannoli and then lowered the window and threw the remainder out. "Fucking expensive way to feed pigeons," he said with a sigh.

Wright waited.

The proprietor hooked a finger on the steering wheel. "I must be out of my mind."

"I know I'm out of mine," Wright said.

The proprietor dropped the finger. "OK, do you want to have a conversation that stays in this car, never leaves it ever? And understand if you say yes, it's like saying it in blood."

"Yes."

The proprietor slipped the car into gear, and they slowly drove away. "I talk better when I drive," he explained, his eyes straight ahead. "I knew her by the name you did, phony, because I checked. I checked everywhere, and I never got her real name out of her, like she was ashamed or afraid, I don't know which, maybe both. But for a while her name was Feoli. Honorary, but it could've been permanent. She was family. My sister treated her like she was her own. That was when she was thirteen, fourteen. Then we lost her."

He went silent. Wright looked at him. "What do you mean, lost her?"

"Shut up, I'll do the talking." His eyes were wet.

They drifted into Somerville and out of it, back into Boston by way of the Charles River Dam. Feoli threaded his way onto Storrow Drive, the traffic heavy for that time of day, backing up in places, and he got off it as soon as he could. He said, "She was a clean kid, never brought no shame to us, even after she left us."

"Please," Wright said in a bone-dry voice, wishing for a glass of water. "I still don't have a clear picture. You're giving everything in pieces."

"That's the way I talk. You don't like it, you don't have to listen."

They were on Commonwealth Avenue, cruising past venerable brick buildings. A young woman was sunbathing on a lower-level roof, sitting with her head back and her shirt off, her hands hiding her breasts.

"Look at that," Feoli said indignantly. "She should get busted. That's something Polly never would've done."

"You called her Polly?"

"That's right. She was my honey, and she knew it." Feoli shot Wright a sharp glance. "I never laid a hand on her, if that's what you're thinking. But I'll tell you something. She was scared I might. I could see it in those eyes of hers. Like I reminded her of somebody who maybe done something to her once. Fact is, she was scared of everybody when we got her."

"Please, tell me about that again."

"She comes wandering into my place looking like a runaway, which was what she was. What else could she have been at that age? Except she was different. She didn't look like she was living in the gutter and fucking with dope. Otherwise she wouldn't have got through the door."

"If she was a runaway, how was she keeping herself?"

"I'll tell you how she was keeping herself, friend. Living in an abandoned warehouse until she got kicked out and then under a God-damned bridge, living on fucking potato chips and little half-pints of milk. Saving her money. She had about thirty bucks, but she was scared because winter was coming."

Wright was about to say something, but Feoli made a fast turn, through a red light, and honked at a driver slow to make way. They were still on Commonwealth but now traveling in the opposite direction.

"What I'm saying, friend, is she comes into my place and looks at everything I sell but orders only a glass of milk. I'm watching, see, and I know this kid hasn't eaten right in a long time, and she's not like the crowd of bums I don't let in the door. This kid's neat and clean, despite how I told you she was living. This kid could break your heart because she don't want to take the cannoli I had the waiter bring her because she thinks she's got to pay for it. She just wants her milk, like a little kid."

"You talked to her."

"Sure I talked to her. Wouldn't you? It wasn't right, a kid like that on her own. Even when she knows she don't have to pay for the cannoli, she still don't want to take it. So I call my sister in Saugus, and I tell her I got somebody I want her to meet. My sister you'd have to know, a good woman, with a heart this big but nothing to fill it with. She don't know what the hell I'm talking about, but she comes anyway, and I'll tell you something, friend. She was the best thing that ever happened to this kid. She takes the kid home and what's supposed to be temporary, just till the kid gets on her feet, becomes permanent, more or less. You see, she's good for my sister too. Two people who didn't have nobody. My sister never married, like me."

They had driven in a circle and were now moving toward Cambridge Street. Feoli jolted the Chrysler from one line of traffic to another, sounded the horn furiously as he made an illegal turn, and then, as if exhausted, pulled over and parked near a branch of the Boston Five, its logo a big buffalo nickel. He kneaded his forehead, as if to squeeze away a headache. Wright stared at the buffalo nickel.

"Your sister died."

"Cancer, in the worst place a woman can get it. She never got any breaks in life. The kid was turning fifteen when it happened. She took it bad. She cried, but she didn't say nothing. That was Polly's way."

"And that's when she ran away from your sister's house, after the funeral."

"She didn't run away. She just left. I wanted her to stay there, with a housekeeper to look after her, but she was afraid, maybe of me. I hate to think that because she had no reason. I was living there too, at least that was my legal residence, but I was never there. She could've stayed, no problem."

"Where'd she go?"

"I don't know. I told you that before. But I made sure she had money before she left, and every six months or so she'd show up in the North End, come to my place, to let me know she was all right, and I'd make sure she had money, even though I had to fight with her to take it. You know something, friend, I'm tired." He rubbed his eyes, the one with the lazy lid the longest. His face had taken on a gray pallor. Suddenly he laughed. "If the Feds drive by, they'll think I'm planning to rob this place, with you helping me."

Wright, only half hearing, said, "All the time Paula lived with your sister, she must've mentioned something about her past life."

"Friend, whatever she told my sister, my sister didn't tell me, like it was between them two."

"You said Paula never went to school in Saugus. Why not?"

"How could we send her? She was a minor, so we shouldn't have had her in the first place without telling somebody, and how could she get into school? You've got to transfer records or something. My sister took care of her schooling. Taught her all the Italian operas, and even took her to some, New York a couple of times. What d'you think of that?"

"Did your sister ever work in Sears, Roebuck?"

"Yeah, years and years ago. How'd you know that?"

"Paula mentioned something about Sears."

"Yeah? Well, it don't matter now. Enough talking. I told you I was tired."

Feoli put the Chrysler into motion and swung back onto Cambridge Street, heading toward the North Station, driving much more carefully than before. He glanced at Wright.

"How's the arm?"

"It's OK."

"Then why aren't you moving it?"

Wright moved it, to show he could, and winced.

"I've got plenty of those in my time. Put ice on it when you get home."

They glided into the lot near the North Station and stopped near Wright's car, which had a broken headlight and little pieces missing from the grill. Someone had backed into it. Wright said, "I appreciate everything you've told me."

"You do? Good. Don't bother me no more. And remember, this stays between us."

Wright used his good arm to push the door open.

Feoli said, "Something I didn't tell you because it doesn't do us any good, but last December, maybe a couple of days after the last time I saw Polly, a guy comes into the place asking for her, but not by name. He describes her to one of my part-time people who don't know from nothing but mentions it to me later, how some guy, maybe a father, comes in looking for a girl. Except my guy can't remember nothing about him, except maybe he's forty, maybe he's fifty."

"He never came back?"

"No, and I kick my ass I wasn't there. I would've remembered him."

Wright walked toward his car, and Feoli drove out of the lot. As he turned onto Nashua Street, he noticed a very young federal agent sitting in a parked tan Dodge, government issue. The agent smiled. Feoli closed both eyes.

Wright watched the Chrysler disappear and climbed into the Cutlass, for the moment too tense and preoccupied to start the motor. Then he became aware that someone was standing beside the car and gazing at him through the open window.

"How about lunch, Mr. Wright?" Spence said. "I know it's late, but I have the feeling you haven't had any. How about on top of the Pru?"

"I'm not a tourist."

"I agree. Instead, how about a place called Friday's on Newbury Street?"

"How about finding my daughter?"

Spence produced a piece of paper and passed it to Wright. "That's the registration of the gentleman who hit your car."

Wright crumpled it up. He started the motor.

"Do you mind if I get in," Spence said.

"I do," Wright said and drove off.

The agent in the back of the van tore his headset off, scrambled into the driver's seat, and sped toward the center of town, wildly looking for a public telephone. He phoned Cogger, who said, "Slow down, what's the matter?"

"I think Oliver zapped himself."

"Holy shit!" Cogger was silent for a second. "You sure?"

"I'm pretty sure. He and his wife were having this fight, and the gist of it is she said she had to get away from him for a while, maybe a long while, and she was going to pick up their two daughters from somewhere and take them with her. I saw her drive off. Then later I heard him messing around in the bedroom, as if looking for something. And then I heard the noise. It sure as hell sounded like a gunshot."

"OK. Get back there. Get into the house. If he's only wounded, call an ambulance and stay with him. Don't let the locals know. If he's dead, don't let anybody in the house. Just wait there. In either case we've got to get those microphones out. We're on our way."

The agent raced back to the van. Cogger, his hand shaking, misdialed twice trying to reach Spence.

13

The man hunched over his plate in the Pewter Pot on Tremont Street, eating hash topped with poached egg, which he saved for last, manipulating his fork around and under it. When the waitress approached to ask whether he wanted anything else, he glanced up with a small greasy smile and stared into the adolescent face framed by pinned-back hair. His throat tightened. "More coffee," he said, barely getting the words out. Her slim arm was taut as she poised the pitcher to pour, and he nearly stuck his hand in the way.

He flushed.

All the waitresses were adolescent, and he could not stop looking at them, his gaze ranging from one young bottom to another, soft edible bodies in identical dainty skirts so short his stomach constricted. His waitress was whispering to another, and he imagined the whispers were about him. He paid his bill and left.

He crossed the Common, climbed steep stone steps and emerged onto Beacon Street, a poisonous smell in the air from traffic which, though drifting now, had been backed up too long. His car was parked on the shady side, and he squirmed into it, rolled down the windows, and dropped his head back, as if to doze, the lines in his forehead relaxing, a hand in his lap. His eyes were shut for no more than a minute when he opened them with a jerk of his head, sensing danger, as an animal might. A meter maid, three cars away, was working toward him, and he took her in all at once: the blue cap perched on the blond bob of hair, the full round face, the plump body squeezed into official clothing. From that distance he tried to guess her thoughts by her eyes. Then he looked toward his meter, which needed feeding. His car was slow to start, which was normal, and he simply kept trying. The panic set in when the motor coughed, gasped, flooded and stank.

She placed a hand on the window ledge and peered in at him, not speaking, not smiling. He could not take his hand from the key, and he continued churning the motor while blinking at her, his necktie askew, his face lopsided from a silly smile. She was younger than he'd thought, and the hairs on her forearm flashed red in the sun. Perspiration stained the underarm of her shortsleeved shirt. He could smell, or thought he could, her powder, deodorant, secret sprays.

"Lay off it!" she shouted, and for a humiliating moment he misunderstood her. Then he let go of the key. He could not speak. His throat, chest and stomach had tightened to a degree that he could scarcely breathe, and his head was full of noise, like the gentle clapping of several pairs of hands.

"Couldn't you smell the gas?" she said, as if he were stupid.

"Waiting for my wife" was what he wanted to say. "Waiting" was all he managed, and he stirred, his body creaking inside his metal-gray suit, which appeared cracked where it was wrinkled, tarnished where it was thin. She was staring down at the suit, and then, as if she did not like what she saw, she returned her hard gaze to his face. "Waiting," he said in the same desperate voice.

"Better take care of the meter," she advised and moved off smartly, obviously to avoid the headache of further dealing with him.

He did not leave the car, and he did not move a muscle while watching her departure in the rearview. Then, slowly, his shoulders slackened, and he waited. He waited until he felt the time was right and then counted carefully to fifty before twisting the key. The motor kicked over and caught on the first try, though still stinking of gasoline.

He drove not to Route 2 but to 93, and he drove well under the speed limit, as if searching for a hidden pass, a peaceful valley. His head was quiet now, and his fly, loose before, was closed, his tie tightened, his shoulders squared, as if he'd been freed from one spell and put under another. Glimpsing himself in the rearview, he saw eyes like stones and a jaw like an iron blade. He turned off at Exit 15.

He drove by woods, a state forest, and saw a bicycle flung by the roadside, the rider no doubt in the woods answering a call. The town was not unfamiliar to him, and he anticipated the white houses that soon burst out of the landscape, then the smaller ones, much lower to the ground, ranches and splits of varying colors, half hidden by ornamental evergreens. As he neared the center of town, the houses crept closer to the street and became big and white again.

A girl at the Gulf station was on her knees drilling air into a tire, and she rose when he pulled up at the far island of pumps. She had a loping stride. Her hair was long and flaxen and her greasemonkey's outfit stained, but her face was fresh and shiny except for a smudge.

He imagined her body a white streak and her breasts small and perfect, disappearing when she lay flat on her back. He saw her navel as a mere pinch and fixed her age at seventeen, or eighteen, though he easily could imagine her younger, barely pubescent. She spoke, and he delayed answering, acting the long-distance traveler, dog-tired, gray in the face, red eyes registering nothing, which gave him more time to take her in. He imagined her young pubic hair crushed against his hand.

"Sir," she repeated.

His voice broke strong: "Ten dollars regular."

She busied herself, and he counted his money, plucking out a ten-dollar bill, which didn't leave him much and didn't bother him. He listened to the drone of the pump and enjoyed the smell of the gasoline.

"Don't see many girls doing this job," he said when she returned to him, and she smiled faintly, accustomed to the question. He tilted his head. "I have a daughter your age."

"You do? What's her name? I might know her."

His mouth trembled only a little. "She doesn't live around here," he said, his tone melancholy. The girl wanted to be paid and extended a palm, which he stared at with enormous interest. He had once weeviled a splinter from Patricia's palm, soiled from play as this one was from work.

"Mister, what's the matter?"

The lines in his forehead were fissures, and his eyes looked bloody. He held the money up, but she was reluctant to reach for it. His hand was shaking, and the bill fluttered. "Please, take it," he said, as if it were candy.

He drove to Parker Street with a vague anxiety and idled the motor near the rooming house, as if Patricia were still alive and living there. He glanced at the spot where he had stood for glimpses of her. After a couple of minutes, he drove away, as if he had just missed her.

The first two times the car cruised past the house, Merle was on the telephone with her father, who was trying to talk her into something. "No, I can't," she said, and he turned silent. He was a retired lawyer, trained in silences and speeches, weighted pauses. As a girl, when she had wanted to do something against his wishes, he would say, "OK, let's plea-bargain and see what we come up with." Remembering this, she started to weep.

"Honey," he said.

She instantly brought herself together and said, "I don't want a terrible lot from life, Dad. Only my daughter back and reasonable dreams at night, no more nightmares."

"I know," he said helplessly, "but, please, at least consider what I said. Arizona isn't that bad, and the heat's so dry here, so different from New England. I know you'd enjoy the desert. Even if only for a couple of weeks, honey. Your mother would love to see you."

"She still doesn't know, does she?"

"No. She's spending half her time in the oxygen tent."

"Oh, Dad."

"Don't fret. Her condition's stable, her spirits are fine." He hesitated. "It's you I'm worried about."

Merle, standing in the kitchen, leaned against the counter and spoke with her eyes shut. "You know, I'd like to be a child again so that everything that has happened won't happen."

"Honey, how about it?"

She opened her eyes. "I can't go to Arizona. It would take me that much farther away from Marcie."

He was silent.

"I know what you're thinking," she said.

"Honey, no you don't."

She did not want to break down again. "Dad, I have to hang up. OK?"

She went outdoors and watered some dying flowers. When the car made its third pass, she had her back to the street. She was bent over a bush inspecting a spider, fat and full, black and yellow, its web aluminum wires in the late afternoon sun. The next time the car appeared, slowing as if to stop, she was tramping toward the red maple. The driver's face floated in the open window. It was a face she could not understand. Too much seemed wrong with it, first the hard flat mouth, then the fiery eyes, the slices in the forehead, and then the hair charging up like smoke, as if the inside of the man's skull were burning up. Their eyes locked into a hideous intimacy.

She clutched a thin branch of the maple and screamed.

The car was gone.

Her legs gave, and she went down on one knee, dragging the branch with her. Too much was playing on her nerves, she understood that; and the man she'd seen was a total stranger, she realized that too. All the same, she felt she knew him.

Detective Harty telephoned Chief Tull, and the chief began to sweat, his face tight one moment and slack the next. "Jesus Christ," he whispered and worked open his poplin jacket, which had a loud zipper. Harty's voice was heated. A pitcher of icewater was on the chief's desk, and the chief lifted it and rattled water into a glass. He said, "Are you sure?"

"Yes, of course I'm sure," Harty said.

The chief raised the glass to his mouth and drained it with several hard pulls.

"For Christ's sake, Chief, are you listening to me?"

He sat silent and wooden as the cold water cramped his stomach. He considered the pain punishment. "I don't know anything about it," he said, as if abdicating all responsibility.

Harty's voice hardened. "Get over here, huh, Chief."

It took him a long time to leave his desk. For a while he sat with a thumb to his mouth, as if sucking a cut. The cramps worsened. He glanced at the wall clock: suppertime. On a normal day he'd be going home.

He left his desk with a strange gait, like a skater on ice, and went out to the desk sergeant, who was peeling pages of that morning's *Herald-American*. The sergeant smiled, and the chief said gruffly, "Anything unusual happen I should know about?"

The sergeant shook his head. "No, nothing."

"Everything quiet?"

"Yes, sir. What's the matter?"

"Nothing's the matter," the chief said sharply. "Why should anything be the matter?"

Outside he saw the young officer, the gum-chewer, who was going off-duty. The chief gestured to him.

"Come on. You're going with me."

The chief climbed into the rear of his car, and the officer slid in behind the wheel and looked into the rearview with an excited smile.

"What's up, Chief?"

"Don't know yet."

"Where're we going?"

The chief gave him the address, number and street, and said, "Drive normal."

They stopped at the lights near the library, a delay the chief welcomed, and he played with the thought of leaving the car to browse for a book, perhaps one on Charles Manson. He had not yet read *Helter*

Skelter, but it had long been on his list. He was almost inclined to reach for the door, but then the car moved, and he flopped back with a pained face, as if trapped in a role he no longer wanted to play.

The officer turned left at the Gulf station, past the Ballardville Bowling Lanes and near boys loitering on the sidewalk. One of them, with a mustache too blond to be effective and spare arms hanging out of short sleeves, challenged the chief with a sneer. The chief leaned to one side, his breathing labored, and silently relieved his sudden anger and his cramps through flatulence.

"Can you tell me what's happening?" the officer asked, with a quick glance over his shoulder.

"Nothing's happening."

The officer, offended, gave a shrug and made another turn. The chief's eyes were closed. He was trying to think about anything except where they were going. His wife had made a large crab salad for supper, which would keep. There was a Charles Bronson movie on TV at eight, and he would surely miss the beginning and maybe the middle. When he opened his eyes he saw the familiar house.

"Jesus Christ!" the officer said. "What's happening here?"

"You stay in the car," the chief said.

Scraping his voice together, the chief said, "Then he's dead."

"He's a God-damned bloody mess," Harty said.

The chief swallowed, gagged a little, and fought for his breath. He and Harty were slouched in lawn chairs behind Oliver's house, where the dying sun cast a red gloom over the grass. The chief had a blinding head-ache, as if he had been short-circuited.

"He's more dead than he needs to be," Harty said. "I didn't know a God-damned little twenty-two-caliber toy could do that much damage."

The chief coughed and said, "Bobby Kennedy was killed with one."

Harty was silent, his expression severe, his eyes on Oliver's house, where federal agents were still poking about.

The chief put a hand to his mouth. "Did he leave a note?"

"I can't hear you," Harty said irritably.

The chief dropped his hand and repeated the question.

"No note, but that doesn't mean there wasn't one. For all I know, he could've written a ten-page letter. I still don't know how the Feds got on top of this so fast and why they practically sealed off the house. It took them a God-damned long time to let me in, and for a while I didn't think they were going to. Then later that zombie with the glasses, Spence, showed up acting like everything was a big mystery to him, which is a crock of shit."

"They've been interested in Oliver," the chief offered diffidently.

"Yeah, I knew that. How did you know?"

"Sources."

"Sources, huh. Well, the Feds fucked up. You don't need sources to tell you that."

The chief looked confused. "But it must've been Oliver who did the thing at the Wrights' house."

Harty snorted. "If the Feds still thought that, they'd be tearing up the ground looking for the kid's body, and they'd have been on the Six O'clock News telling us all about it. Case cracked. Another one for the G-men."

The chief swallowed, settling deeper into his chair, as if intending to spend the night there. "But why did Oliver kill himself?"

Harty looked at him with parted lips and what may have been a smile. "You asking me, Chief? Ask the Feds. I'd like to hear their answer too."

The chief thought of supper, of Charles Bronson. Of John and Merle Wright. He said, "I made a promise to the Wrights."

"Shouldn't have."

"It's not absolutely certain their daughter is dead."

"Let's put it this way, Chief. Years ago when I was a trooper, a little girl was missing, last seen at the bank of the Merrimack River, one of her shoes found in the mud. There's only one conclusion, right?"

Harty rose. The chief wanted to, but he was afraid his legs wouldn't support him. Finally he made the effort and tottered, his eyes smarting, an explosion of mosquitoes around his head. Harty, who had taken a few slow steps, glanced back.

"You all right?"

"My stomach."

"Ulcer?"

"Maybe."

"You take things too personal, Chief. You never should do that."

Harty's stride was lumbering, and the chief hurried to catch up, slipping over the grass. Oliver's Pinto was parked in the drive, with somebody sitting in it.

"Who's that?" the chief whispered.

Harty gave a glum glance at the car and said, "Oliver's son. He won't go in the house. He's waiting for his mother."

The chief stared at the boy, whose eyes had a

crushed quality from crying. His mouth was closed and looked as if it might never open again. The chief said, "Where's his mother?"

"That's something else you'll have to ask the Feds. They're looking for her. Seems they're doing your job for you. Nice of them, huh?"

The chief caught Harty's sleeve. "You mean she doesn't know yet?"

"Your guess is as good as mine."

The chief took a step toward the boy, as if to console him, but Harty flung out a hand, almost a punch.

"Leave him alone."

After a solitary supper she merely picked at and then a long soaking bath she didn't want to leave, the woman lay on the couch and watched "Starsky and Hutch." Her favorite was the young blond man with Slavic cheekbones. For a season and a half she had thought he was Starsky, not Hutch, but now she had them straight. She tried hard to follow the story line about a woman who was a file clerk during the day, a prostitute at night, and then a victim of a murder. Her mind, however, was elsewhere. She was listening for the sound of her husband's car.

She dozed during the news and dreamed that somebody, a doctor, was lovingly touching her cheek as she lay with her legs spread and strapped in stirrups, for she was giving birth to one baby after another, each by a different man, and the doctor was waiting for his. She woke up weeping to a loud commercial, Bob Hope wearing a hard hat and shilling for Texaco.

Drinking tea at the kitchen table, she told herself there was no need to worry, for this was hardly the first time her husband had absented himself for a long block of hours, and all day at the hospital she had anticipated coming home to a deserted house. She tried not to question the wisdom of what she had done to the photograph album, but her thoughts kept moving in that direction. Her tea went cold.

She went to bed but did not sleep, and after a couple of hours she got up and stood by the window looking out at the web of moonlight caught in the black tree. At times she seemed to sleep on her feet. At dawn she began systematically searching the house for the remains of the album to see whether she might be able to restore it.

14

In the night he heard a crack and then a great sweep of breaking branches and knew that somewhere a dead tree had fallen. Raising himself on one elbow, he scratched mosquitoes from his face. Later, nearly asleep, he heard fierce screams from the vicinity of the water: a small animal or a bird being attacked, killed, eaten. He pulled his suitcoat over his head and slept badly.

He woke with stinging eyeballs and for a while kept only one eye open, as if that were the only way he ever saw life, through a peephole. Climbing stiffly from the car, he was chilled by the air, the ground, the damp of dawn, the sodden trees that needed several more minutes before being ready for the world. While urinating, he listened for voices. Campers were in the woods, though none near him, most on the far side of the pond near the swimming area.

His suitcoat over his arm, he followed a rutted dirt road to an inlet, which was coated with duckweed and lily pads. He looked for signs of a kill at the water's edge but saw only the remains of a condom, the rubber ring. He stared at it for a time and then moved to another spot. Stripping to the waist, he washed away the blood from bites on his face and neck. The water was rich and rank with odors, like a secret brew out of a fairy tale. Strangely, he felt less of a chill with his upper body bared, and then no chill at all as the sun came upon him. He picked blueberries for breakfast.

He made his way along the pond, stumbling at times on tough aerial roots that snarled out of trees and hung out traps, but the going grew easier when he reached a footpath bordered by heavy clumps of fern. The smell of leafmold was pervasive. When he came in sight of a hexagonal blob of blue nylon, he stopped short, as though the breath had been taken out of him. Then he crept quickly off the path and lay on his side behind two small pines.

Presently a bare-legged woman wearing a man's shirt emerged from the tent and went behind bushes. He could see pieces of her through little leaves but not enough to matter. Then she strolled down to the pond and entered the water up to her ankles. Seconds later two children, a girl and a boy, both towheads, rushed out of the tent in swimsuits and charged toward her, direct and together, as if to smash into her. Only at the last instant did they veer apart and skin by her, throwing themselves into the languid water. He waited for a man to appear, but none did.

When the three of them left the water and converged in front of the tent, he closed his eyes and listened to their chatter, which had a hypnotic effect. He felt he could stay there forever if only they would. Burning charcoal soon singed the air, and later came the aroma of coffee, then of bacon. The chattering subsided, and he let his head loll. The narcotic sun was feeling its way into his clothes. His weight rested on his right arm, and his hand was going to sleep. Then, through the fuzz of his brain, he heard a small voice and jerked his head up, his eyes bloody stains. The boy's eyes stood out, polished oversized pennies flashing through pine needles.

Agent Spence, who had not invited them, welcomed them coolly and allowed them to occupy chairs in front of his desk. His face was blank, as if he were capable of strangling all emotions, and his posture was rigid, as if he were not merely an investigator but the absolute head of a secret organization with no visible chain of command, no hierarchy, no significant memos. While seeming to view none of his visitors directly, he took in details, including the tiny repeated patterns in John Wright's conservative necktie. Merle Wright, though still striking, was drawn and hollow-cheeked. Chief Tull had shed his poplin jacket for a plaid polyester sports coat that didn't fit properly, and he was no longer carrying the Magnum. His jaws were hacked from shaving, and his whole presence was curious, like that of a suspicious and uncomfortable chaperone. He had pulled his chair almost behind the Wrights, as if he wanted them as a buffer.

"If there's a connection, we'd like to know it." John Wright was doing the talking, and Spence listened with cold eyes. Unaccustomed to being interrogated and annoyed that Wright and his wife had lighted cigarettes, he became more aloof and for a while did not provide an ashtray.

"You could give them the courtesy of an answer," the chief said abruptly.

Spence did not bat an eye, and he spoke so low he

forced them all to lean forward. "His connection was with Miss Aherne, not with your daughter, Mr. Wright."

"What was that connection?" Wright asked.

"He knew her better than he'd let on."

"Would you care to be explicit?"

"The man's dead, Mr. Wright. I assure you there's no need to go into it." Spence shifted his eyes to the chief, who felt obliged to speak.

"We were under the impression, at least I was, that he was a prime suspect."

Spence folded his hands together and placed them under his chin. "Where did you get that impression, Chief? I'd be interested."

The chief shuffled his feet, and Spence smiled.

"He may have been your prime suspect, Chief, but he was never ours. We knew from the start we were dealing with a weak individual no more capable of committing a violent crime than your mother or mine."

"But you were working on him. Trying to break him."

"Chief, that's language out of a movie. We don't go around trying to break people, but we do seek the truth, and Oliver was obviously not telling us everything, criminal under the circumstances. I think we can all agree on that."

"Why did he kill himself?" Merle asked, her eyes dark and direct. "Did you let him think he was a suspect?"

Spence unlocked his hands and regarded her indulgently. "Mrs. Wright, I couldn't begin to guess what went on in that man's head. I think I've made it clear he was unstable."

Merle's eyes flashed. "I can't help thinking it comes down to a game, even right this minute."

Spence's indulgence vanished. "That's insulting, Mrs. Wright. Also, you interrupted me. Add to Oliver's problems the fact his wife was leaving him."

"Did you locate her?" the chief asked urgently.

Spence turned slowly and said pleasantly, "Yes, we did, Chief. She and her two daughters are at her mother's house."

"What about the boy?"

"He's there too. An agent drove him. The mother lives in Wakefield."

The chief appeared grateful, as though the boy had been his responsibility and the FBI had relieved him of it. John Wright lit a fresh cigarette and said, "So what you're saying is that Oliver's death has no bearing whatsoever on what has happened to my daughter."

Spence suppressed a sigh. "Yes, that's what I've been trying to say, Mr. Wright. At the most, had he been candid with us, he might have put us a little closer than we are now to the real criminal."

"Where does that leave your investigation?"

"Ongoing."

Wright strained to read Spence's face. "Can't we relax the rules?" he asked.

"What rules?"

"I feel as though we're working under some," Wright said.

Spence assumed a bemused look. "You've become very complicated, Mr. Wright. I'm afraid I don't understand you."

"No," Merle interrupted, rising. "We have both become very uncomplicated people with only a single thing in mind. We want our daughter back." She used a long pale hand to sweep her hair from her forehead. "We won't waste any more of your time."

Wright got to his feet, and the chief rose into a stiff

and unnatural stance. Spence did not try to detain or hurry them but stood like a gentleman and then at the last second stepped around his desk to escort them to the door and to hold the chief back.

"Could I have a word with you?"

The chief glanced quickly at the Wrights and said, "I'll be right with you."

Spence closed the Wrights out and kept the chief in, and he smiled slightly. The smile looked manufactured, the tool a knife with a keen blade. He said, "You've got nothing to worry about."

Blood rose up the sides of the chief's neck, and for a moment he had only a rippled image of Spence. "What do you mean, I've got nothing to worry about?"

"Just that, Chief. Nothing else."

The chief was silent, as if on advice from a private voice that sounded warnings and urged him to leave, but Spence held him with the smile, the same smile Spence had used years ago when ordering a man to his knees at pistol point.

Spence said, "I don't want you to think you owe anybody an explanation."

"I don't," the chief said and wished he had said nothing.

"You seem upset."

"I'm not. Why should I be?"

Spence adjusted his glasses. "You were merely doing your job. As you saw it."

The chief did not want to ask what Spence meant. He knew what he meant and experienced a burning under his heart. Spence placed a hand on his shoulder.

"I think you've been doing a good job," Spence said, his glasses reflecting light and spinning like wheels. The chief tried to back off and get away from his hand, but Spence held him, not with a grip but with the smile again. "I was wondering if you'd do something for me," Spence said.

"What?"

"You're chummy with the Wrights, which is smart. Good police procedure. You're the good fellow. We're the bad."

The chief did not want to nod, but he did, and at the same time he said, "They're good people. They've lost everything."

"No, they haven't. They've got you, Chief."

"What do you mean?"

"They're stumbling around, trying to do our work. It's rather pathetic but of course understandable, perhaps even natural. But thank God they've got somebody like you keeping them in sight. Protecting them, you might say."

"Yes," said the chief, feeling better, though not much better. The burning sensation had risen through a good part of his chest. He wanted to mop his forehead, but Spence's hand was in the way.

"What I'd like, Chief, if it's not too much trouble, is for you to keep me posted on what they're doing. You never know, they might luck on to something." Spence lengthened his smile. "Well I don't want to keep you."

Spence's hand faded away, and the chief reached for the door, uncertain whether he had committed himself.

Traffic in the North End was immobilized as if by a strike, a constant clutter of cars on streets not really meant to accommodate anything larger than pushcarts, some streets unusable because of double-parked cars, others because of delivery trucks. Spence leaned an elbow out the window and said, "Quaint, isn't it? Guineaville. What it needs is urban renewal."

Cogger, his foot playing with the brake, said nothing. His new wife was Italian.

"We should've walked," Spence said. "Park when you can."

"That might be even harder," Cogger said and then with surprise pointed to a crowded fruit and vegetable stall on Spence's side of the street. "Look at the size of those bananas that woman is buying."

"These people eat big. They don't get tall, but they spread out. See that stuff in the box near her. Do you know what it is?"

Cogger craned his neck.

"Squash flowers," Spence said. "They fry them in a deep batter and press them into patties. Get your wife to make you some."

"How are they?"

"You have to acquire the taste."

Cogger inched the car forward. "My wife probably wouldn't know how to make them. She's not a real Italian. She's not even Catholic."

"I gathered that," Spence said, consulting his watch. "See if you can squeeze into that place up ahead."

"No way."

"Do you want me to try it?"

"OK, I'll try."

Twenty minutes later Spence and Cogger entered the coffee bar and peered at customers. Business was brisk, with several waiters working. Spence looked coldly at a whining boy whose mother was trying to ignore him. Cogger whispered, "He's down there."

"I know."

"I don't think he's seen us."

"Of course he has."

They weeded their way toward the rear, where Feoli

was sitting with an elderly cardplayer who was snapping an ace. The cardplayer, without looking up, scooted his chair back and went to the men's room.

"Gentlemen," said Feoli.

"You mind?" said Spence.

"Be my guest."

Spence sat down, and Cogger remained standing because there was no chair for him. Spence said, "Nice place you've got."

"You oughta try my cannoli. Special recipe."

"Don't want to spoil my supper."

The young waiter appeared and stood near Feoli. Spence gave him a short glance and said, "Nothing, thank you." The waiter remained. Spence gave him another glance and said, "What are you looking at?"

"Nothing," said the waiter.

"Then go clean a table. This is private."

The waiter didn't move, and Feoli smiled and said, "Do what the man says, Nicholas." The waiter drifted off, and Feoli said, "They don't show respect nowadays, do they?"

"That's how they get hurt."

"My thoughts exactly." Feoli sat back, interlocking his heavy hands behind his head. His left eye fluttered. "What can I do for you?"

Spence shrugged. "This is all friendly. I came to see your place. I didn't realize you had such a thriving business. Good customers. Families, kids. A lot of kids. You must like kids."

"Sure. Don't you?"

"I don't have any."

"I don't either." Feoli dropped his arms and laid his hands on the table. His smile was almost sweet. So was Spence's.

Spence said, "That's right. You never married."

"Who needs it?"

Spence used both hands to delicately adjust his glasses. "By the way, I'm sorry if that fellow Wright has been bothering you. We told him to stay home, but he wouldn't listen. Stubborn, I'm afraid."

"Hey, don't worry about it. I feel sorry for the guy, his wife too. You guys haven't been able to do much for them."

"These things take time," Spence said, "but he's not making our job any easier. He and his wife think they're a couple of detectives, which puts a burden on us."

"Is that right?"

"You see, we don't take them seriously, but we have to pretend. You know, go through the motions."

"Must make it rough on you."

"Rough on other people too," Spence said. "You see, he and his wife were in my office today, and he made some pretty wild accusations about you. You see my problem?"

Feoli's left eye closed.

Spence smiled.

"Like I say, I feel sorry for the guy," Feoli said.

"I'm sure you do, and I feel the same. That's why I'd like to clear this thing up fast, for your sake, I mean. Easiest way would be for you to take a polygraph."

Feoli's left eye opened. "Kiss my ass."

Spence's face whitened, and he twitched once, no more. Cogger edged closer to him. Two tables away, the young waiter stared at them. Spence said, "You know that this place is being watched on other matters. Don't be surprised if that surveillance intensifies."

"I'm being watched? I didn't know that. Thanks for telling me."

Spence lifted his chin. "I could put this place out of business in a week."

"Hey, I could use a Florida vacation."

Spence rose, his face hard-looking, as if it had the texture of a seashell. Cogger straightened his shoulders.

"No hard feelings, huh, fellas?" Feoli said.

"That wasn't good," the young waiter said.

"What d'you mean, it wasn't good?"

The waiter shook his head. "No matter how you cut it, it wasn't good."

"Hey, I asked you?"

"I'm just giving you my opinion."

"You think he's going to do anything? He's going to do shit."

"You shouldn't of pushed him."

"What are you, a lip-reader?"

"I've got eyes."

"You got a cock too. Go play with it."

The waiter picked a hair off his sleeve. "And I don't think you told me everything."

"That's right. I never tell you everything, and you're lucky I tell you anything. Who the fuck are you?"

"We got a good thing here. It would be bad to lose it."

"You let me worry about it, OK? Go get me a coffee."

Chief Tull, his tight sports jacket riding up in back, entered the station, nodded glumly to the desk sergeant, and said, "Anything happening?"

"Not much," said the sergeant, peeling a page of the *Herald-American,* seeking the crossword puzzle.

The chief, eying entries in the log, struggled out of the sports jacket and slung it over his shoulder. "What the hell is this?" he said suddenly, planting a heavy finger on the log.

The sergeant leaned sideways for a look and said, "Oh, yuh. A woman, one of the campers in the state forest, came in to complain about a man exposing himself. Had two kids with her, boy and girl. She said he did it in front of the boy. Nice woman. Comes from Melrose."

"You got Malden here. Which is it?"

"What's written there, that's what it is," the sergeant said, leaning over again. "Yuh, Malden. I get those two mixed up."

"You get a description?"

"Ah, you know how kids are. And the woman didn't really see him, except the back of him when he was running off. The kid did say he had funny hair and dents in his forehead. Gray hair, he said." The officer paused. "Oh, yuh, and the guy was in a suit, necktie and all."

"So what did you do?"

"Sent a cruiser there, what d' you think?"

"Turn up anything?"

"Naw."

"Funny hair and dents, huh? How old's the kid?"

The sergeant scratched the back of his neck. "I'd say about nine, his sister a little younger. The mother looked to be about thirty. She packed up and went back to Melrose."

"It is God-damned Melrose or Malden? Jesus Christ, you sure it's not Medford?"

"Chief, I told you I get those mixed up. It's like it's written there."

The chief looked smug. "So we've got a pervert in the woods, huh?"

"That was this morning. I don't think he's there anymore, Chief."

"You don't? Where do you think he is?"

The sergeant hunched his shoulders. "Home, probably."

"How good did we look through those woods?"

"Well, they're big woods, Chief, and, you know a guy exposing himself is kind of common."

The chief gave the sergeant a sad look. "You don't see any significance in this?"

Ten minutes later the chief was speeding toward the state forest, wearing his poplin jacket and his Magnum.

When the woman returned from work and saw that her husband was still not home, she took a quick bath, put on a good dress and a hat, and went to church. As a child she had considered confession a marvelous thing, so personal, with the priest caring and gentle. The only trouble was that she had had nothing of consequence to confess. During adolescence there had been a few sins, some mortal, but by that time she had wanted to keep them to herself, which, she discovered, was still the case. Blessing herself, she left the church without a word.

15

The path dipped away from Chief Tull, and he got one foot wet in a sandy place. Skipping gingerly to better ground, he encountered two trim middle-aged women with binoculars who mistook him for a game warden until they saw the holstered weapon hanging from his hip. He quickly identified himself, while trying to dodge bright bullets of sunlight that were hitting him in the eye. One woman said, "My God, that's a big gun," and the other said with a smile, "I hope you're not shooting any birds with it." He shook his head solemnly, as if they were children, and rattled them with swift questions about a man wearing a necktie.

"My God, what's he done?" asked the first woman. "Murder?"

"He showed himself," the chief said in a subdued voice, which he then raised. "But he might be a murderer. He's a suspect."

"Jesus, Mary, and Joseph," said the second woman.

They went in one direction and the chief in another, catching hold of a slender birch with a green-yellow spray of leaves to help him up a banking, where he was careful not to trample scattered patches of tiny

crimson flowers. He ate a blueberry. When he entered
a deeper part of the forest where the sunlight fell only
in flakes, everything seemed too composed and calm,
including the choruses of birds, and he touched the
butt of his Magnum just to make sure it was there
and viewed his left wrist for the time, not that it was
important. A bright butterfly blew by him like sparks.
Plunging into leaf and shadow, he experienced a small
but real fear of being swallowed up.

In time he had to pause and struggle for breath, while
clutching a bush of brick-colored leaves and searching
for the blind circle of sun through the trees, as if for
bearings. His heart thumped harder than he felt it had
a right, and his head hurt from unwanted thoughts of
Oliver. He retained but a blurred impression of the
man's face, which became more indistinct, perhaps a
blessing, each time he tried to dress it up.

He tripped on an outcrop of rock but caught himself and waded through brush down a gentle incline.
Making his way around heavy trees, the ground sucking at his police shoes, he stopped short at the sound
of something vague and distant, regular for a while and
then variable. His lower lip quivered. Then, as though
someone had pushed him in the small of the back, he
flopped to his belly. The sound was not as distant as
he had thought.

He lay on ground where it was not really good to do
so, his nose near the pungent odor of moss and the
stagnant sour stuff that lay beneath it. He felt chilled
to the bone, as if he were smelling death, his eyes held
by a small green plant he thought was blowing blood
at him, but it was the blood of berries. Not far beyond
that was a large moist mushroom the size and color of
a sick man's face, everything there except the features.

The sound grew more noticeable, as if something were creeping toward him. His right arm was curved beyond him, the tint of berries on his stark hand. Slowly he inverted his arm and edged his hand toward the Magnum.

By the time he filled his hand and raised himself on one knee, he had determined that the danger lay not twenty yards away, and he brought himself up to a careful crouch and gripped the Magnum with both hands, aiming it at what he still could not see. His finger tightened around the trigger. When the sound ceased, he realized in the instant what he had been hearing all along, but he was frozen in position, geared solely to act. Vaguely he spotted a rising shape and clearly saw a girl's bare bottom matted with bits of leaves and pine needles. Then, as another shape floated up from the ground, he saw everything, things he didn't want to, the girl's meek little face, her rib cage, the boy's bearded chin. The girl looked like one of the waitresses at the luncheonette who served him a cruller, but he knew she was not. The boy looked a bit like his son. He jerked his arms into the air and held the Magnum high over his head.

"Get out! Get out! God-damn you, get out!"

He screamed hard, the weight of the gun bending his arms back to where he didn't want them. For what seemed forever, the boy and the girl stood paralyzed, expressionless, almost as if the two were one, and one shot would kill them both. The boy bolted first, into a thrashing bareassed run. The girl, scrambling for some clothes, followed. The chief reeled.

He sat all at once on the ground, as if his whole body had been stung, the Magnum laid out in front of him like a great bird he had caught in flight and subdued. He thought of his wife's muffins, apple pie, pot roast and of the little things, some of them not so little, that needed repairing around the house, and he tried to remember what was coming up on television that evening.

He was still sitting in the same position when he heard the distant slam of a door, which did not come from the direction in which the boy and girl had fled. A second later he heard the efforts of somebody trying to start a stubborn car, and he listened with the satisfaction of one who usually does not have such problems.

The man drove to downtown Ballardville and purchased a throwaway razor and several candy bars in the CVS store. The young woman who rang up the sale viewed him with a little amusement, as if he were a tramp. He did not look at her. He was rubbing one of his eyes.

Eating one of the candy bars, he parked in the municipal lot, which flanked a complex of stores of neocolonial design, Olde Ballardville Center, young trees growing out of squares in the asphalt. Most of the stores were closing for the day. He wondered what his wife was doing and put her in front of the television or in the tub.

He ate another candy bar, which hurt his teeth, and he smoothed out and folded the orange wrapper and left it on the seat beside him. Though he had not smoked a cigarette in years, he craved one. When it grew dark enough, he left the car and relieved himself behind one of the stores, and when he returned he ate the remaining candy bars.

Sometime after midnight a police officer flashed a quick light into the car. The beam picked up the orange wrappers but not the man who lay huddled in back. The man's head was tucked away, and his suit looked like the seat. He stirred and groaned in his sleep as the officer lumbered off toward the dark stores.

"What's the matter?" his wife asked.

"Nothing," he said and went to the phone and called Detective Harty at Harty's home in Winchester, interrupting his dinner. "Sorry to bother you. This is Ed Tull."

"Yeah, Chief, what can I do for you?" Harty said, chewing.

"I think I've come around to your way of thinking. What I mean is, I agree with you now about the Wright girl. I don't think she's alive either."

"What changed your mind?"

"We've got a pervert loose in the state forest."

"What kind of pervert?"

"He took his thing out and showed it to a boy. Mother and daughter right there."

"Whose mother and daughter?"

"The boy's."

Harty was silent for a moment. "Chief, every forest has a pervert, and some even have hermits. In fact, I suppose you could call a hermit a pervert. When I retire, that's what I plan to be, a hermit. Tell you what, we'll talk about this tomorrow."

"You haven't heard me out, so listen for a minute. I think the body of the Wright girl is buried in that forest."

"Chief, hold on. We had a lot of people comb those woods, and I mean *comb!* And if I remember rightly you weren't one of them because you thought we were wasting our time."

"Now I think different. And I can probably give you the general vicinity of where to look in those woods."

After another small silence, Harty said, "How do you know that?"

The chief faltered and then said roughly, as if speaking from a raw throat, "From a source. OK?"

"What source?"

"Can't say."

"What the hell are you giving me? You're not a reporter. So what are we talking about?"

"Please," the chief said breathlessly. "Trust me on this."

"I want to know what information I'm acting on. Chief, I just haven't got time to go into things blind."

"I was out in those woods today. Call it intuition if you want, but I know what I'm talking about. Have you ever felt something in your bones and muscles and everything else. Well, that's the way it is with me about this."

Harty mumbled something and then said, "Do you know what it'd be like trying to get a backhoe into those woods and what it'd cost?"

"It'd be worth it."

"Chief, call the Feds on this. Better yet, get yourself a shovel."

The chief lowered his voice. "Do you know what you are? You're a prick."

"Chief, I've been called worse things."

Then Harty disconnected.

Merle Wright did not know Barbara Oliver well, but she put her arm around her and said, "Thank you for letting us come."

"Thank you for calling."

The two women stood together like sisters. Barbara Oliver's three children and her mother were seated in folding chairs just out of earshot. The casket, a caramel presence against a float of flowers, was closed. Merle tried not to look at it.

Barbara Oliver said, "I don't like this place. I called the first one in the book. I didn't know what else to do."

"I think you did well," Merle said, as John Wright stepped closer to them. Barbara Oliver seemed to see him for the first time, though he had kissed her cheek moments ago.

She said to Merle, "I don't think I could have borne your loss."

Merle was silent, but she strengthened her embrace, aware of the heavy silence of the Oliver children. The two girls had lowered their heads. Barbara Oliver stared into Merle's eyes.

"He didn't have anything to do with it. If he had I'd have known. Do you believe that?"

"Yes," Merle said, and she did, fully.

Barbara Oliver looked at John Wright with eyes that definitely were not seeing much. "Do you?" she asked.

"Yes," he said.

She swayed a bit, as if Merle's embrace had grown uncomfortable, and Merle dropped her arm. She said to Merle, "I'm not sure how happy his childhood was, but none of us has a perfect one, do we? Nor a perfect marriage."

"No," Merle said.

Barbara Oliver leaned back a little, squinting toward her children, as if to reassure herself they were there. Then her earnest face cracked into a terrible smile that affected her voice. "I wasn't leaving him, you know. I was only getting away for a while. He must have known that."

The odor of the flowers was reaching Merle, along with all the moist colors, as if the flowers were blossoming in her face. They watered her eyes, blurring Barbara Oliver, except for the awful smile.

That night in bed Wright put his arms around Merle. They had not made love since their daughter had disappeared. When he started to draw away, she said, "No, I want to."

They did so without words and almost without kisses, absorbing each other only in the primal way, a slow pump, as if repairing damage, tightening flesh, strengthening bonds, getting themselves together after too many mangled weeks. The kisses came after they increased their pace and her hands gripped his taut arms to keep them from buckling.

When he came out of the bathroom and rejoined her under a damp sheet, she said, "He wiped her out."

"I know."

"He left her with a guilt she'll never get over."

"She might be stronger than you think."

"Nobody's that strong."

"We are," he said.

"Are we? What are we doing, John? We're chasing a ghost trying to find our baby. We're searching for poor Paula as if she were alive."

Wright said nothing.

Merle rose on her knees, naked and enamel in the near-dark, and peered down at him. "John, don't ever wipe me out."

Spence was about to leave for the day when Cogger burst into his office and said, "You won't believe this! Honest to Christ, you won't!"

"Yes, I will," Spence said, sitting down behind his desk. "Make me happy."

"Remember our Mr. Feoli used to have a house in Saugus? His sister lived in it, and he spent time there?"

"Keep talking."

"Well, first of all, in case you didn't know, his sister died."

"You're not telling me anything."

"I want to put this in perspective for you."

"Sit down," Spence said. "That way I can hear you better. The sister died a couple of years ago, and twelve years ago his brother was fished out of the river. I know that. Get to the point."

Cogger squashed himself into a chair and grasped the arms, as if to keep himself there. He took a breath and said, "All of a sudden, say about five years ago, somebody else is also living in that house, some kid who doesn't go to school like she should, and not an Italian kid either. This girl's blond and maybe about fourteen years old then. Neighbors don't see much of her, but they catch glimpses of her, enough to know she's non-Guinea, and they hear the woman there, the sister, call her Polly."

Spence let himself slide back, just a bit. "Keep talking," he said.

Cogger went on for perhaps a half hour. When he finished, he took out a handkerchief and wiped his face and neck. Then Cogger smiled. "Shall we haul him in?"

Spence also smiled. "I've got a better idea. Let's just drop a little of it on him, and then we'll walk away and watch him sweat. You'd be surprised what could come of it."

Toting shovels over their shoulders, Chief Tull and the young officer climbed the banking. The shovels were brand-new, paid for out of the chief's own pocket at Hill's Hardware. He could have requested shovels from the Public Properties Department, but he had not wanted to explain his need for them. His step was sure and steady, his eye keen. "Watch those flowers there," he instructed.

"What flowers?"

"For Christ's sake, you stepped on them."

The young officer muttered something behind the chief's back, the chief scraping past high blueberry bushes and leading the way like a jungle soldier with more than his share of combat. His poplin jacket bore yesterday's stains from the forest floor. When they reached the high trees that blotted the sun, the officer said, "It's creepy here."

"Bet your ass it is. Perfect place. Leave the blueberries alone." The chief trudged on, glancing back again a few minutes later. "Look out for the rock."

"Jesus Christ, where? Where you got rocks, you got snakes."

The officer tripped on the rock anyway and nearly fell. The chief forged ahead, holding his shovel now like a rifle, using it down the gentle incline to butt away branches and bushes and occasionally bugs.

"Hey, Chief," the officer hollered. "Let's stop and rest."

The chief, puffing, had already stopped. He was where he wanted to be, standing on the spot where he had lain yesterday, looking down at crushed berries and rich mosses. The shovel in one hand, he abruptly went down on all fours and sniffed for death. The officer rushed to him.

"Chief, what's the matter?"

The chief hoisted himself up with his shovel and said, "Nothing's the matter. You start here."

The officer peered down at the spot. "Jesus," he said, perplexed. "Nothing's been buried there. I mean, that ground hasn't been touched in a hundred years, maybe never. I dig, the only thing I might find is an Indian."

"That so."

"I don't know if we've even got a right to do this. I mean this is state property."

"Dig."

With an exasperated sigh, the officer dropped his gun belt and billy and flung his cap. The chief ambled to where the bearded boy and girl had had their fun, and he stared at the sodden clothes left behind. He stared at the girl's tiny underpants, flimsy bra and tattered sneakers. She had grabbed only her shirt and shorts. The boy had left everything, including probably his wallet. Idly he wondered how the boy made it home.

The officer pounded the ground with his shovel and hollered, "Jesus Christ, Chief. It's all roots."

The chief kicked the clothing to one side and struck his shovel into the ground, hitting rock. He tried again.

"Chief, if I'm going to dig, at least let me dig where there's hope of finding something. What I'm doing here is trying to fight a tree."

The chief kicked the clothing farther to one side and struck again. This time the shovel sunk into the soil. He began digging down hard, his face furious and dripping, the handle of the shovel tearing skin off his right palm. When he stopped to lick it, he saw the officer hatefully regarding him.

The chief set his face before speaking. "OK, try somewhere else."

"No," the officer said. "What's happened is I'm about one breath away from telling you to take my badge and shove it up your ass."

The chief was slow to hear the words and then slow to make sense out of them. He had soil in one of his shoes and a slight gut pain. Finally he said, "Get out of here. Take your shovel and wait for me in the car."

He labored alone with a clumsy strength, with a handkerchief wrapped around his hot right hand, stumbling from one place to another, the tough ground frustrating him and pushing him farther afield. Every so often he detected noises and considered the possibility of being poleaxed. The pain in his gut worsened. There was a break in the trees, and the sun scorched him, which made him stop and shake his shoulders. The handkerchief had come loose and hung from his raw hand. His face was a big bruised apple. Suddenly he strode toward a tree and viciously swung the shovel at it, the blade biting the bark and drawing juice. Then he hurled the shovel into a brush, finally seeing the folly of his work, though still unshaken in his belief that a small body was buried somewhere in the forest.

"Please," he said.

Merle Wright stopped with a jolt in the Purity Supreme lot, her arms around a heavy bag of groceries that nearly spilled. The voice: she recognized it and she didn't. It was behind her. She spun and faced what looked like a derelict who had brutally shaved himself

THE BABYSITTER • 195

and now needed a dollar to get him through the day. Then she remembered the car, his face.

"Please, let me talk to you," he said, his voice solemn, stubborn, yet broken.

She knew instinctively it was not money he wanted. He seemed beyond that. He seemed moribund, his face spent and stricken, pulverized around the eyes, as if he had just taken his knuckles out of them. It was not his eyes that held her, but his voice. She wanted to hear it again.

"I know you were good to her," he said.

"Who?" she said, her heart pounding. The groceries were hurting her arms.

"She was good in school," he said. His eyes were haunted.

"Who?" she said, knowing who. "Are you talking about Paula?"

"Patty," he said, speaking now in almost a falsetto.

"Paula," Merle said, crying. She wished she were not alone. "I'm sorry," she said, awkwardly freeing a hand to wipe her eyes. "I understand, I do. Paula is Patty. Is that right?"

He didn't answer, and she sought to read what was shot into his face, despair perhaps and a fatigue that was total. He seemed to have trouble staying on his feet.

"Please," she said. "Was Paula, Patty?"

He seemed to nod. She couldn't be sure, and she couldn't stop the tears from coming again. He was crying too. "Here," he said.

He jammed something into her hand, and she immediately began spilling things. "Oh, my God!" she said and dropped everything except what he had thrust upon her, a torn color snapshot held together by transparent tape, the face of a child of seven or so, with the eyes and smile of Paula Aherne. She tripped over groceries. "Where's my baby?" she said, trying to grab him and grabbing nothing. He was gone.

She heard the sound of a car taking its time starting and somehow knew it was his car, but she couldn't determine where it was. Holding the snapshot in both hands, she wandered from one car to another and found hers but not his.

16

On the third day the woman stayed home from work, setting up the ironing board in front of the television. She watched "For Richer, For Poorer," "Card Sharks," "$20,000 Pyramid," "High Roller," "Wheel of Fortune" and, with trepidation, the noon news. She ironed curtains, sheets, and the white uniforms that made many patients mistake her for a genuine registered nurse. Before making a light lunch, she telephoned a co-worker at the hospital to find out how things went with Mr. Bullard. Mr. Bullard was an eighty-year-old man scheduled against his will for transfer today to a nursing home. Yesterday she had needed to take his wrists to break his hold on her. The co-worker did not know how things went with Mr. Bullard, only that he was gone.

While eating her lunch of packaged soup and crackers, she watched "Search for Tomorrow" and admired the decor of the room the characters conversed in. She put extra sugar into her coffee by mistake but drank it anyway. After cleaning up, she felt a weariness, along with a churning—a need to rest and to get her bearings. She ran bath water.

In the mirror she saw worried eyes, a set mouth and slumped shoulders. Looking down, she saw the flash of a childhood scar on her foot, and in memory she saw the child, then the burgeoning adolescent; she saw the wary eyes of each, each betrayed too many times. She stuck the foot into the tub. She lay with her head deep in the water, only part of her face showing, her hair drifting.

She woke gradually, her back aching and her shivering body more naked than before. The water was gone, drained out, and her hair clung coldly to her head. There was a scratching at the window: rain coming out of a half-darkness. She raised a sore arm to clasp the side of the tub, and her face dissolved into a groan. She called for her husband.

The ringing was at first vague, then plain, and she groped her way toward it while trying to fit an arm into her bathrobe and then giving up. The bathrobe fell between her legs and she reached for the phone. "Hello," she said hysterically.

"Hello." The voice subdued her. It was male and authoritative, and it belonged to a stranger. She felt despair mounting. "Mrs. Leszkiewicz?" the stranger said, pronouncing the name imperfectly.

"Yes," she said, her face fixed.

Spence entered the coffee bar alone, the crowded hour, voices pitched high, the reflective espresso machine registering his presence. The young waiter appeared. Spence, speaking low, almost with a smile, said, "Move out of the way, turd."

Feoli stood talking to a table of women with cool pleasant faces and spoons poised near their ice cream. He talked to them longer than he intended and longer than they wanted. Then, without acknowledging Spence, he moved toward him as if to pass him. Spence stood with his arms at his tailored sides, a straight and impeccable figure in a gray lightweight suit, his glasses screwed securely onto his face.

"Come on," Feoli said from the corner of his mouth.

Spence followed, in step.

They took a table for two in back, and Feoli said, "What the fuck is this. You almost look sociable. You like me now?"

"I never disliked you," Spence said. "Not personally, although sometimes it may appear that way because of my line of work. I also want to apologize for the other day. My associate and I shouldn't have burst in on you that way. I'm sorry we did, but you understand, I trust."

"Sure. I love you too. You want to try some of my cannoli now?"

"No thank you, but I'll tell you what looked good. That ice cream those women were eating. Usually I don't touch sweets, but what the heck."

Feoli threw up a short powerful arm and snapped his fingers, the sound like a shot. An elderly waiter responded. Spence smiled at him.

"Strawberry ice cream, my man. Little dish."

"Give him a big dish," Feoli said. "I don't mind if he wastes it."

"Little dish, please. Waste not."

Spence and Feoli exchanged lazy smiles. Feoli said, "What else can I do for you? Want a cigar, one that don't stink?"

"Oh, no. I haven't smoked in years."

"Same here."

"Then we have things in common, I see."

"I could've told you that a long time ago."

Spence pursed his lips, as if conceding a point. Then he assumed a faintly pained expression. "Another thing I want to say is, I never had a chance to offer condolences when your sister passed away, when was it, a couple of years ago? Three? That's a nice town, Saugus. My associate lives out that way, next town over." Spence put his hands on the table. "Anyway, you have my belated sympathy."

Feoli's right eye was blank, the left one hooded. With a small flourish the elderly waiter set a silver dish of ice cream near Spence, who said, "Hmmm," and dipped a delicate spoon into it. Feoli said, "That ice cream gets mentioned in magazines."

"I believe it. Delicious."

"Tony Spinazzola writes for the *Globe* mentioned it."

"That makes it official," Spence said and took time to pat his mouth with a napkin. He smiled.

"Should've got the big one," Feoli said.

"Oh, no. I'd become an addict," Spence said and spooned away the last of it. Again he used the napkin, small deliberate pats.

"You got nice moves," Feoli said.

"Pardon?"

"Look, I ain't got botulism of the brain. You got something to drop on me, do it, get it over with. I got a business to run."

Spence, saying nothing, displayed a mask of innocence, with his glasses as perfect eyeholes.

"We playing cat and mouse? That what we doing? Want me run under a table?"

"I came in here to relax," Spence said. "You're not letting me."

Feoli gave him a fierce one-eyed stare. "OK, you've had your ice cream. Now get the fuck out."

"If I weren't careful about my weight," Spence said pleasantly, "I'd have some more. You see, that's your problem. You don't watch yours."

"That's right," Feoli said, as Spence took his time rising. "Lot of things I don't watch."

"That's how things come back to haunt you," Spence said.

"Pure and simple," the waiter said. "He's got a hard-on for you."

"No shit," Feoli said. "He's had that for years."

"But now you got your legs open and can't close them. Go 'head, try. You can't."

"You worry too much."

"Maybe you don't worry enough. You were wrong about the Wright guy. You told him those things, you should've cut out his tongue first."

"Maybe, I don't know."

The waiter shook his head. "I don't know how you figure things anymore."

"You don't have to know."

"I'm thinking you don't figure so good as you used to."

"Nicholas," said Feoli with a murderous smile. "I'm tired of your mouth."

"I'm saying these things so you'll figure good again, if it ain't too late."

Feoli shrugged. "The other day he came in here he had nothing. He came in like an actor, and I could tell he had nothing the more I thought about it. He was only throwing out lines about the Wright guy. Today was different, and one of the lines I didn't like. Meaning maybe he's got a little something."

"Maybe more than a little," the waiter said.

"More than a little, I wouldn't be standing here shooting the shit with you. He'd have come down on me like gangbusters, and you could've been saying I told you so even louder."

The waiter shook his head. "I don't know. I think he knows how to figure things on his own, with or without the Wright guy, and doesn't matter if what he figures isn't exactly right. We still get hurt."

"We don't get hurt," Feoli said. "*I* get hurt."

Chief Tull, sitting at the Wrights' kitchen table with a glass of ginger ale, listened carefully. The taped snapshot of the young Patty or Paula lay near his fingers, and Merle Wright's voice swelled around him, too softly, too airily. Her cigarette smoke floated in front of him. She was trying to control her emotions and was too calm. "Yes, go on," he said, lifting his glass and catching the sting of the ginger ale against his nose. "I hear you."

Her husband said, "She didn't actually see the car. She heard it."

Merle said, "I'm not absolutely sure it was his, but I *feel* it was."

"It was his car all right," the chief said strangely, as if peering far over their heads. He did not seem excited. He seemed, in fact, a little sad. "Everything is falling into place," he said.

The Wrights stared at him.

"You know the car?" John Wright asked.

"Oh, yes. But like your wife I've never seen it. I was close to it once, but not as near as your wife got. And she came face-to-face with him. I haven't done that."

"Who is he?" Wright said.

"I don't know," the chief said dolefully, as if wishing now he had told them nothing.

Merle said, "It was the same voice I heard on the phone."

The chief said offhandedly, "The FBI still has the tape. We could ask them to play it, to make sure."

"I *am* sure," Merle said, and she pointed to the picture. "And that little girl is Paula."

The chief reexamined the picture. It seemed to pain him. He said, "It stands to reason the man might be her father."

"No, I don't think so," said Merle. "Nothing of her was in his face."

"Stepfather then, or something else."

Merle nodded and shivered at the same time. She lighted a cigarette, her husband holding the match. He said, "How do you know about this man, Chief?"

"Just simple police work, Mr. Wright. Nothing more."

"Chief, what are you holding back from us?"

The chief looked tired, a little ill. "Nothing. A complaint came in about a man in the woods. I went looking for him. After a while, I got to thinking I was chasing a ghost, but your wife proved he's real."

"How do we know it's the same man?"

"The car, Mr. Wright. The car." The chief's voice had risen, as if he were the one who needed to control his emotions. "I hope I'm wrong."

"What?"

"Sorry," the chief said. "Private thoughts."

Wright shuddered inwardly from thoughts never totally suppressed since Marcie had been taken, from questions he dared not ask. The reality of rapists who ravaged babies. Sexual madmen. If his daughter was dead, he prayed she had not died that way.

Merle said, "Maybe the man's still in those woods."

"What woods?" Wright asked with scarcely a voice.

"State forest," the chief said quietly. "No, I don't think he's there anymore. If I did, I'd still be there."

"He was desperate," Merle said. "He was trying to tell me something with his face and with this picture of Paula. Now he's gone somewhere, maybe for good. Now he's a ghost again. Like Paula."

Merle's eyes were wet. John Wright said, "I think we should tell the FBI, and that state detective too."

"You can do that, Mr. Wright."

"Or what, Chief? You were going to say something else."

"I don't think they care much about us," the chief said quietly. "They're political people. Nice fellows and all, but not like you and me."

"Then what should we do?"

The chief was silent.

"Chief, what's wrong?"

He looked at them both. "Give me a day. Let's see what I come up with."

"You don't look good," his wife said.

"I don't feel good," said the chief.

His wife, bending over him, stroked his forehead. He was stretched out on the couch, shirt and pants loosened, shoes off. The television was tuned low.

"You should go to bed," she said.

"No, I'll just stay here for a while," he said, his eyes closed.

She let him sleep.

A half-hour later the phone rang, and she scrambled for it and got it on the second ring. It was for him, and she was insistent with the caller about not waking him, but he was already awake and groping toward her, rubbing his thin hair back and tightening his pants. He grabbed the phone and said, "Yuh."

"Chief, I was told to call you."

"Yuh," the chief said, recognizing the voice, an officer from the graveyard shift, an old-timer.

"The sergeant said you wanted to know if any of us seen any strange cars around town past few days and to contact you right off if we did."

"Right," the chief said, trembling.

"I seen one. Last night. Well, this morning really, a little after one in the municipal lot near the fancy stores. A junk that shouldn't have got an inspection sticker. I flashed a light on the tires. Back ones were bald. I flashed inside the car too. Full of candy wrappers on the front seat."

"Just sitting there."

"Right."

"Don't suppose it's still there."

"Nope. I checked before I called."

"Don't suppose you remember what kind of car, make and year."

"Big old Pontiac. That good enough?"

"Don't suppose you wrote down the registration number."

"Nope."

The chief quietly and savagely cursed.

"I never write 'em down," the officer said. "Don't have to. I remember 'em for a week, and then I forget 'em. I figure a week's long enough."

The chief gestured crazily to his wife for a pencil and pad. "So you remember this one," the chief said offhandedly and held his breath.

"Sure."

The chief's son came home, a tall gangling youth

with uncut hair and a heavy foot. The boy entered the room hollering to his mother about something to eat, and the chief shook his fist at him to shut up. The boy made a surly remark and vanished.

"OK," the chief said, juggling the pad and readying the pencil. "I want you to give it to me real slow, one number at a time, not in bunches."

The officer cleared his throat and recited the numbers, which came across to the chief like a countdown in code, an explosion to follow. He recorded them in a slow and quivering hand.

"Massachusetts?" he asked.

"Right."

The chief's sigh was pronounced. He said to the officer, "You going on duty tonight?"

"Right."

"You've got a reward coming. Take the night off."

"Might be better if I checked the lot to see if the car comes back."

"Don't sweat it. I'll do it."

"I've got nothing else to do."

"OK, we'll both do it," the chief said irritably and hung up. Then he was smiling, but the smile didn't last, and he felt a chill in of all places his underarms and crotch. His wife looked at him inquiringly. "I think I'm in business," he said.

"Isn't that good?"

"For me maybe," he said, "but maybe not for the Wrights."

The man left Ballardville by Route 495, which was fragmented by repair work, flares, flashing arrows, road-narrowing barricades of barrels, construction crews, trucks, state police cars. It took him through

Tewksbury, Lowell, Chelmsford, and Westford to Little-
ton, where he picked up familiar ground, Route 2.

He drove with his mouth firmly set, seemingly ab-
sorbed by the rush of the road, and with both hands
on the wheel, as if the car had a will of its own and
might try to steer him to places he didn't want to go.
To orchards in the town of Harvard, where as a boy
he and others had traveled by truck from Gardner to
pick apples, so much a basket but nothing at all if the
fruit was bruised.

The sky began clouding up, and he noticed a sudden
wind pushing at a field, as if to force it from one
property to another. The road swelled, rose, because
the steep side of a hill, and he increased his speed,
strained the motor, heard it knock and skip. The air
sharpened, cutting away much of the day's heat. It was
ready to rain, a gray rubbery sky. He made the hill
and coasted. When the road leveled off, he accelerated,
and the car vibrated.

He passed signs he didn't need to look at to read,
signs for Fitchburg and Leominster, marked with the
miles to come. It was afternoon, but now it looked like
evening, as if special events were to take place, a cur-
tain dropping. He flicked on the headlight. A glance
in the rearview showed himself smiling, for what reason
he didn't know and didn't care. Cars raced by him,
sleek vehicles that soon shot out of sight. The needle
of his speedometer jiggled, wasn't accurate. A flashing
state police cruiser zoomed by, perhaps after those
other cars. Or perhaps he was the target, and the
trooper had merely overshot the mark. He strained to
see whether the cruiser was waiting up ahead for him.
His lips twitched, and he remembered his large foolish
mouth trying to capture the growing child's small con-

torted one and succeeding. The first drops that splattered the windshield reminded him of the heads of dandelions exploding into dust.

He rode into the rain and accelerated as if to get out of it, the vibration worsening. His window was wide open, and the rain gusted in, soaking his arm, shoulder, neck, the side of his face, his hair. Then the front of him, like a bath, a cleansing. The windshield was a wave now, a terrible weight on the wipers, which couldn't work the way they wanted to, and the headlights played tricks in the rain, creating illusions of smoke and sparks, exploding cinders, like stuff flying out of a furnace. He tried to raise his window and found it stuck. He looked for the road, which was leaving him, melting away, exposing in its wake rugged boulders and rainsoaked trees.

He thought of his wife.

The crash was godawful, a hideous sound, as if everything along Route 2 were coming apart.

17

"Mrs. Leszkiewicz?"

"Yes," she said, her face fixed, her head cricked back, her bathrobe at her feet. He identified himself. Trooper Rogers or Roberts, calling from the hospital. She listened carefully to his deep-chested voice, while her mind raced ahead and finished his words for him. She said, "Is he still alive?"

"Yes, ma'am, but you should get here as soon as you can. If you don't have transportation, I can arrange it."

"Then he's not going to make it," she said, amazed at her serenity.

The trooper was silent.

"You can tell me. I'm a nurse."

He stayed silent.

She said, "That's an answer, isn't it?"

"I guess so, ma'am. Do you want me to send somebody for you?"

"No, that's all right." She looked toward the window. "How long has it been raining?"

"Quite a while," the trooper said after a pause. "Ma'am, you don't have much time."

She cradled the phone and bent for her robe, but the

reach was too much. Her fingers missed it, and she moved along without it, bumping furniture, her stride short and jolting. The living room needed picking up, but the task exceeded her strength.

She watched the six o'clock news to see whether her husband was on it, but he wasn't, which made the telephone call seem unreal. She changed channels. When the telephone rang again, persistently, she thought it was part of "Mary Tyler Moore," but the characters also ignored it, puzzling her. Then Ted said something silly and made her laugh.

And then cry.

She did not cry long, as if her body were reluctant to do anything except shiver. With much effort she moved from the couch to the soft chair her husband usually sat in, immediately feeling his warmth, detecting his odor. She sat with her naked legs pinned under her and with her arms wrapped across her breasts, her face tranquil. She was shivering only a little.

She dozed.

For a long while, her eyes opening and closing, she listened to a mysterious sound she felt wasn't meant to be fathomed, but gradually the sound took shape and turned quite loud, quite urgent. Still she ignored it, for what she thought was many minutes but in reality only seconds. The television was still on, and she turned it off, though not without glancing at what was on, a movie. Then she glanced toward the window, her hand going to her hair to fix it. It was raining, not hard.

She opened the door.

The trooper was huge, a giant, much younger than she had supposed, with a square jaw and startled eyes. "Yes," she said, her expression polite and ready to become attentive and even cheerful, as if she wanted to make trouble for no one and wanted no one to make it for her. The trooper, shod in glossy leather boots, seemed to step back into the rain without moving, while his jaw jutted out.

"Mrs. Leszkiewicz?"

Again he mispronounced her name, and this time she gently corrected him. His cap sat squarely on his large head, and she liked the way his hair curled over his forehead beneath the visor. She thought of him as a son.

"Your husband died," he said, staring down at her.

"Oh my God!" she said, as if the voice had just woken her. She began to weep.

"Ma'am," he said. "You go get some clothes on, and then I'll come in."

"I'll get it," John Wright said and picked up the phone.

"How are you, friend? You know who this is, so I don't have to tell you?"

Wright, recovering fast from his surprise, said, "Yes."

"Good, keep it that way."

"I'm glad you called," Wright said, as Merle came close to him and listened in. "I think we—"

"Friend, let me do the talking, OK. A little point, something you can clear up for me like a good fella. Remember the Boston Five?"

"The Boston Five? Yes, yes of course."

"That stayed confidential, didn't it, like it was supposed to?"

"Yes, except for my wife."

"Friend, the truth."

"I swear to God."

"Yeah, that's what I thought. Dumb of me to call."

"Listen," Wright said, smiling at his wife. "I think we've finally gotten a break. Remember that fellow you never saw, the one that came into your—"

"Friend, don't say nothing like that on the phone, OK? That's why it was dumb of me to call. I'm getting fucking senile."

"All right, I understand. But I thought you'd be interested in this."

"Friend, it ain't like I'm not interested. I wish you and your wife all the breaks. I hope you get what you're going for and become a family again, you know what I mean? But me, I got to tend to business."

"I want to thank you."

"Don't thank me."

The line went dead, and Merle stepped back. Wright put the phone down.

Merle said, "What was he telling us?"

"I'm not sure," Wright said, "But I think I can guess."

Chief Tull, removing his poplin jacket from a crinkly drycleaner's bag, said to the desk sergeant, "The Registry get back to us yet?"

"Not yet, Chief."

"Shouldn't be taking them this damned long. They've got computers now."

"Maybe all those old hags they got there don't know how to run 'em," the sergeant said, inspecting the point of his pencil, gearing up for a crossword.

The chief shrugged on the poplin, shifted his shoulders around in it, and zipped it up a little bit. He dusted his police pants and looked down at the shine on his shoes. "I'm going to get a cruller. You call me there if it comes in before I get back."

The sergeant didn't hear him. He was taking a call. The chief had walked a few steps when the sergeant smothered the mouthpiece and beckoned him back with a wink and a whisper.

"Your friend the Fed."

"I'll take it in my office," the chief said.

He took his time. He closed the door quietly behind him and, sitting at his desk, straightened a few things on it. He coughed deliberately, and he ran his hand over the phone before snatching it up.

"Yuh," he said, stretching his legs.

"You sound like a busy man," Spence said.

The chief laughed. "Not so you'd notice."

"I've been expecting to hear from you."

"Nothing much happening here," the chief said, with a cough.

"How are your chums doing?"

"My chums?"

"The Wrights."

"They've been staying put."

"You mean they're staying away from Little Italy?"

"Little Italy?"

"They have a pal here in Boston, the North End."

"I don't know too much about that."

"You wouldn't be holding back from me, would you, Chief?"

"I've got nothing to hold back," the chief said angrily.

"Easy," said Spence. "Don't be so touchy. We're all working together, aren't we?"

"I've got more on my mind than just the Wrights. I've got a whole community here to take care of."

"Maybe I phrased that question wrong, Chief. Maybe they're holding back from you. That's possible, you know. As I said before, we don't want them getting hurt."

"I don't think you have to worry about that."

"My nature, Chief. Can't help it. The same as I worry about you."

"I don't want you worrying about me. You don't have to."

"Chief, I know that. You're a big boy. We're all big boys." A tiny pause. "Chief, somebody's trying to get me on my other line. Why don't you give me a buzz tomorrow after you've had a chance to see the Wrights again."

Spence disconnected before the chief could respond, and the sudden stillness of the chief's office had a stinging effect. He replaced the phone and slunk sideways in his chair, no more appetite for a cruller. His hand dangled toward a drawer. He groped inside it, pulled out something that looked like candy, and tossed a Tum into his mouth. Last night he dreamed he was in combat with a large animal, a fight to the finish in a deep part of the forest, and he emerged the winner with his own hands, but at what a price, at what disfigurement. The memory of the dream increased his discomfort. Then a slight noise put him on the alert, and he was ready to fight again.

The sergeant had opened the door and was looking in on him with a small smile. "I've got what you've been looking for," the sergeant said, coming forward with a slip of paper.

"Read it to me."

The sergeant squinted at his handwriting and said, "Walter something. Maybe you can say it. I can't." The sergeant started to hand the slip over.

"Spell it," said the chief.

The sergeant did, holding the slip close to his eyes, and then said, "One of those Slavic races, maybe even Russian. Lives at 22 Fuller Street."

"No Fuller Street in Ballardville."

"This is in Gardner."

"Where the hell is that?"

"Past Fitchburg. I had a friend bought furniture there once, genuine colonial."

The sergeant laid the slip down, and the chief glanced away, somber for no apparent reason. "Get me Gardner PD," he murmured.

"Sure, Chief, but what's the matter?"

"Everything's falling into place."

He stayed in his office, door closed, and took over the call, talking to a man who sounded like himself, which for a number of moments made him question the call, the badge on his shirt, the existence of the sergeant outside the door. His left hand, freckled and pale, lay flat on the desk, and he studied it. Then he coughed, picked up the slip, and said, "Let me spell that last name for you, L-E-S-Z-K-I-E-W-I-C-Z."

The voice in Gardner picked up on the spelling and said something the chief had to take time to decipher, for the voice was a little hoarse, like his own sometimes. Then he stiffened in his chair.

"Oh my Christ!" he said. "You're kidding!" The voice indicated otherwise, and the chief began jotting details of the accident on the back of the slip the sergeant had given him. "Let me have the trooper's name," he said, giving his forehead a good rub. Then he sprang a few more questions and listened with his head lowered.

After he cradled the phone, he slid down in his chair and stretched his legs under his desk as far as they would go. He had more than once taken a nap in that position and wished he could take one now. The sergeant looked in on him again.

"Any luck?"

The chief opened his eyes. "They said it rained out that way yesterday."

Spence said, "I'm getting more than I expected."

"You deserve it," Cogger said. "You've waited a long time for him."

"The Boston Five. That can mean only one thing. In one way or another he got money from Wright."

"That's the way I read it too," said Cogger, "except we know Wright's bank account. What's he got, a couple of thousand dollars? Feoli's out of his league."

"Not necessarily. How long have we been watching him? At least a month before the Wright thing broke, and during that time nothing's been going down. He could be very hard up."

Cogger nodded. "True."

"What happens to a guy like that, you see, is he starts thinking small, and when that happens he becomes stupid and careless. That phone call, for instance. Feoli said it himself, *dumb.*"

"Right," said Cogger.

"However,'" said Spence, smiling, and tipping back in his chair, "I've already checked with the bank in Ballardville. Wright hasn't touched his savings. And he has no account at the Boston Five."

Cogger cocked his head. Spence removed his glasses and commenced cleaning them with a tissue. Cogger watched and then said, "So where does that leave it?"

"Leave it? Leaves it right where it was, I'd guess." Spence fitted his glasses to his face and deposited the tissue in the wastebasket. "We can't assume Wright has only two thousand dollars to his name, not when we know he and his wife worked a number of years at one of your better advertising agencies. They must have pulled down pretty good salaries, with only themselves to worry about. I wouldn't be surprised if they invested in stocks and bonds."

"Have they?"

"I don't know yet, but I mean to find out."

"That means Feoli could've gotten them for a bundle. Pure con job, unless you really think he's mixed up with what happened at the Wrights' house."

"That's a messy situation there," Spence said with a glance at his watch. "And almost beside the point, if somebody off the street did it."

"Is that what you think now?"

Spence smiled. "Let's say I'd like to think it."

"Maybe we ought to have somebody start watching the Wrights' house again."

"Can't spare anybody. Besides, we've got the chief for that."

Cogger grinned.

Spence said, "When are you going to get him to cut my grass?"

"So he's dead," Merle said, as if she had known he would be. The chief nodded, and Wright put his hand on her shoulder. She said, "He might not be the same man I saw."

"I think he is," the chief said. "When I talked to the chief in Gardner, I didn't tell him why I was so interested, passed it off like it was traffic violations, but I managed to ask a few questions. The chief there's like me, knows his town, and he seemed to remember that some years back the Leskywicks, or however you say it, had somebody with them, like a ward of the state, a little girl they took care of. He said he guessed the girl was grown now and living on her own, not in Gardner. I didn't say anything."

The Wrights were silent, poker-faced. Merle took a small sip of ginger ale but didn't seem to taste it, as if she had merely wet her lips. The chief took a healthy slug of his.

Wright said, "Is there a child in the house now?"

The chief put his ginger ale to one side and cleared his throat. Merle closed her eyes. The chief said, "He told me no, Mr. Wright. He said it was just Mr. and Mrs. Leskywick living there."

Merle opened her eyes. "You have the address?"

"I thought you'd ask that, Mrs. Wright, but first let me tell you something. Afterwards I called this Trooper Roberts who investigated the accident, and he said the man just drove his car right off the road. No skid marks and no reason except the rain. Anyway, he later went to the house, and he said Mrs. Leskywick had a funny way of showing her grief. He called her a basket case."

"I have to see her," Merle said.

The chief looked at John Wright and picked up his ginger ale glass. "You know that bourbon you offered me one time? How about throwing a little in this?"

Wright went to the cupboard and brought back the bottle. The chief held up his glass, still half full of ginger ale, and Wright said, "Want me to throw that out first?"

"Just pour it right on top."

Wright did, and he did the same to his glass and to Merle's. The chief took a hard swallow, and his eyes watered. For a moment he looked miserable. He coughed.

"Maybe now," he said, "is the time to call in the FBI, let them handle it."

"No," said Wright. "We've done well without them. I don't want to spoil our luck."

The chief took another swallow and pushed the glass away. He wiped his eyes, then his mouth, and said, "Mr. Wright, it depends on what you call luck. I mean, I think we've got to consider something you and your wife haven't faced." He faltered. "A possibility, I mean."

Merle quietly lit a cigarette, and Wright looked at his drink. He said, "Would anybody like ice?"

The chief glanced away, his thoughts turning to himself, to the small red forest flowers that might have bloomed and died unnoticed had he not happened along, his presence a good thing. He felt his presence here, however, a sharp intrusion.

"What I'd like you to consider, Mr. Wright, is that going to Gardner might not do you people any good. We're getting pretty close to this thing now, and, well . . . Mr. Wright, maybe you and I ought to talk alone."

"My wife knows what you're saying."

The chief gave her a quick glance.

"We'll concede the possibility," Merle said in a bone-dry voice.

The chief let his gaze settle on Wright and said, "Figuring the worst, the absolute worst, the man could have . . . could have left your daughter anywhere between here and Gardner, a place we might never find. We've got woods everywhere, and there's a chance he did what he did without his wife ever knowing it."

The Wrights said nothing, and the only sound was the give and take of the chief's breathing. He appeared devastated. The silence grew until finally Merle picked up her glass.

"When do we leave for Gardner?" she asked.

The chief sighed. "We ought to give the woman a chance to bury him first."

"When will that be?" Wright asked.

The chief propped a hand on the table. "I'll find out," he said. "Then we'll all go."

18

Two women she knew from the hospital accompanied her home from the funeral, one older than she, the other youn er, both solicitous and willing to spend a little time with her, into the evening if necessary, but she said she wouldn't mind being alone.

"May, are you sure?" the younger woman asked.

She nodded, the lines in her face relaxed.

When the younger woman started to speak, the older one signaled against it. Then, perfunctorily, they took turns embracing her, the older woman last.

"May, you call if you need anything. Do you have my number?"

She nodded. She stayed at the door and watched them leave and waved when they glanced back. Then she went into the house and closed the door and moved quietly past familiar things. The only sound she heard was a squirrel that had leaped from the tree to scamper over the roof.

She lay on the couch in the silent room, hunched on her side, her shoes still on, her eyes closed, and watched her husband peel off his socks after a hard day at the furniture factory. She saw him look up at her with a question in his eye, and she heard herself say, not to him, but to herself, "No, I would never hate you. I don't know how." She heard him ask where Patty was, and herself say, "Gone." She tried to sleep, but his voice stayed in her ear.

When she finally abandoned the couch, she considered eating because it was that time to do so. She made herself a little something while setting a tidy place at the table, but she did not eat much. Each time her fork came down too hard on her plate.

In the bedroom she rummaged through things of her husband's in a dresser drawer and found what she was looking for hidden away, an empty envelope from an old electric bill, with numbers penciled on the back, which was all she was interested in, but she absently looked at other things too: the thumb-sized Polaroid picture of him on an expired driver's license, a yellowed membership card from the local American Legion post, a GI life insurance policy, which he had let lapse.

She placed the envelope next to the telephone and dialed the number, then redialed it because she forgot to put a "one" before it. She waited with her eyes closed, expecting an operator to break in and tell her that the number was no longer in service.

"Hello," a woman said.

The voice came at her too fast, and she had to swallow to find her own. "This is May Leszkiewicz," she said.

"How did you get my number?" the other woman said after a moment's pause.

"He had it."

The other woman was silent.

May Leszkiewicz said, "You don't have to tell me why he had it. I know why."

The other woman still said nothing.

"I'm all alone now," May Leszkiewicz said. "I'm a widow."

"I didn't know that. Was he sick?"

"Yes."

"Kind of sudden, wasn't it?"

"Yes."

The other woman was silent again, and the silence seemed angry and then excruciating, as if a bad wound were being opened.

"I didn't call you to cause trouble."

"Then why did you call?" the other woman said, her voice sharp and uneven.

"I thought maybe I could visit you sometime. We could be friends. I always wanted to be."

The other woman almost laughed. "That's impossible."

"I won't cause trouble."

"You said that. And of course you won't. Don't think I don't know why." The other woman took time to get her breath. "I don't want you to visit me."

"We have things in common. We could talk."

"You silly bitch." There was a pause. "I'm making a new life for myself."

Now May Leszkiewicz was silent. The little food she had eaten was not resting well in her stomach.

"I shouldn't have called," she said.

"Don't do it again."

She replaced the phone softly, as if pretending she had never picked it up. In the kitchen she balled up the old envelope and clenched it nearly into a knot before dropping it into the sink and setting a match to it. With fascination she watched it smoke. Then the flame took hold, and it began to blossom.

She switched on the television for the six o'clock news

and lay on the couch to watch it, this time with her shoes off and a pillow tucked under her head. She did not intend to close her eyes, but gradually she did, and when she opened them the news was over, and she had missed the start of the nightly "Mary Tyler Moore" rerun on Channel 56. She certainly must have slept, and she must have dreamed, for she had seen her husband again. In the distance he had looked young but had aged with each approaching step until she threw up a hand to stop him.

She thought of Mr. Bullard and considered visiting him at the nursing home. She consulted her watch. Perhaps she would, perhaps not now, but tomorrow for sure. Now she would take her bath.

"What the hell was that all about?" the man asked, standing near the open window with his shirt off to catch a little breeze, his hands on his hips, as if he occupied a small position of power.

"You better go now," the woman said.

"Oh, I get you," he said, dropping his arms. "You don't want to talk about it. Just like that."

"Keep your voice down," she said. "It's nothing that concerns you."

"How am I to know that unless you tell me what it was about?"

"Put your shirt on."

He approached her. He was neither young nor old and had styled hair. His face was a little chewed by the years. He started to embrace her, and she pivoted away from him. He looked at her with rancor as his hands slid away.

"You're not Miss Alaska anymore, or whatever the hell you were. And for Christ's sake, how many years ago was that?"

"I don't count them," she said, "but you can if you want."

He smiled, not nicely, and patted her belly through her blouse. "What's that? An extra loaf of something?"

She viewed him with a faintly sour expression. This man was starting to remind her of others she had known.

"I need some money," she said.

"Oh, you know how to ask for that, don't you?" he said with more rancor than before. "Don't care anything about holding your hand out, do you?"

He looked around for his shirt, and she pointed to it. He put it on and undid his pants to tuck it in.

"I'll tell you something, sweetheart," he said, changing his tone a bit, though his anger was still there, "you shouldn't bottle up your feelings so much. Doesn't do you any good."

She had nothing to say to that, or nothing she wanted him to hear. She watched him smooth his shirt, which was expensive and colorful, a young man's shirt. He smiled at her.

"You're a funny woman."

"I am what I am," she said.

He took money out of his pocket. "How much do you need?"

"A hundred."

"Hey, come on." He counted out seventy and dropped the bills on a small table. He came to her and kissed her, as a husband might. "I'll see you tomorrow."

"No," she said. "I'd like to be by myself tomorrow. Make it the next day, Thursday."

He wrinkled his forehead. "If I don't see you tomorrow, that means I won't see you till next week sometime. I've got a lot to do."

"That's up to you."

"I have to see my family sometime."

"I said that was up to you."

He studied her. "Maybe I can make it Thursday after all, arrange a few things.

She shrugged.

At the door he said, "Do you want to tell me what that call was all about now?"

"Goodby," she said.

"I may have miscalculated," Spence said. "Maybe the Wrights didn't make as much as I thought."

"Easy to do," said Cogger. "A lot of times those prestigious agencies pay peanuts. No stocks and bonds, huh?"

"Not as far as I can determine."

"What about hidden assets, a bundle in a safe deposit box."

"No, I think we're on the wrong track there," Spence said, dropping back in his chair. "Doesn't matter. But wouldn't it be something if Feoli faked us out on that call? Had a little fun with us about the Boston Five. That's something a Guinea might do because it makes him bigger in his own eyes."

"Wright would've had to be in on it too."

"Possible."

"He doesn't seem the type. And this is too serious for him."

"He doesn't know which end is up and might've thought it was serious and got conned into playing."

Cogger looked doubtful but said nothing.

"What you don't understand," said Spence, "is the mentality of these guys. Wright is an emotional cripple because of what happened to his daughter, and Feoli was born one. That's what we're dealing with here."

"So what do we do?"

"We squeeze a little harder."

Feoli looked up and said, "What the hell are you, family now?"

"Customer. I love your ice cream." Spence sat down and glanced about for the elderly waiter. "Mind if I snap my fingers the way you do?"

"Go ahead. I got five dollars in my pocket says he won't come."

"Don't you usually only carry fifties?"

"OK, fifty."

"You missed my point."

"You didn't make one," Feoli said and didn't smile, forcing Spence to.

Spence said, "I know where there are six fifties that belong to you. The poor kid who had them doesn't need them anymore."

Feoli looked upwards. "Something just went over my head, did you see it?"

Spnece turned his head in a certain way, so that his glasses sparkled. He said, "Those fifties belong in the Boston Five, not with us, Mr. Feoli. We don't pay interest."

"No shit."

"Those fifties tell us a lot about you, almost more than I care to know and certainly more than I need to know. Am I coming through to you yet?"

"Over my head again."

"A lot goes over your head, but that didn't. You're going down, do you realize that yet, and I'm afraid to tell you for how long."

Feoli held out his hands. "OK, cuff me."

Again Spence was forced to smile. "In my own good

time," he said. "I'll have somebody else do it, but I'll watch."

Feoli snapped his fingers, and the elderly waiter appeared. "Get this gentleman ice cream. I want to watch him eat."

They drove into Gardner, past the faded blush of brick factories and down a narrow street that showed the rear ends of small stores, some of which did not seem in business; past an inordinate number of pickup trucks and Volkswagen vans advertising services in crudely painted letters on the doors; past idle men in work clothes. The day was hazy, the sun a stain.

"It's a dismal place," Merle Wright said, her eyes searching for children and finding many, more than she could gather in one sweep. "Slow down, please," she said, and John Wright did.

"It's tucked away from everything, that's all," said Chief Tull.

They were in the Cutlass, Wright with a tightly clenched hand on the wheel, Merle in the middle, the chief with an arm hanging out the window. Downtown was small, cramped and trafficky, and some of the stores had tenements above them, porches hanging out, the architecture industrial, bunches of boxes, the inspiration of a long-ago mercantile mentality. A woman on one of the porches was bent in two, shaking out her washed hair. Merle ran a smoothing hand over her own.

"Let's ask him," the chief said, pointing to a thin figure poised pole-straight at the corner. Wright pulled over, and the chief stuck his head out the window. "Hey, fella, where's Fuller Street?"

A gray-haired man veered toward them. He had

week-old whiskers, the flush of a drinker and the injured nose of one, but he was anxious to help and mouthed directions in a French-Canadian accent, indicating a short drive with a number of lefts and rights, one bent hand showing how sharp each turn was and the other nervously unbuttoning the top of his shirt, his neck too small for his circle of collar. Merle stared at him as if he were God.

The Cutlass slid by a traffic signal as it changed color, while a policeman full of years watched from the curb. The chief, out of habit, waved. Wright made a hard left onto a narrow street characterized by a density of small houses, not all of them kept up, one with the remains of last year's Christmas tree perched on the porch and shedding silver.

"I'm scared," Merle said, "and I didn't think I'd be."

Wright touched her. Then he made more turns, with the chief dipping his head to check street signs. They found Fuller Street.

"That's the name," the chief said, pointing a slow finger to *Leszkiewicz* on a mailbox. Wright pulled abruptly into the drive.

"Careful," the chief said. "The woman's not right. Maybe I should go in alone."

"No," said Merle adamantly.

The chief gazed through the windshield. "By right, you know, I should contact the locals. Tell them what we're doing here."

"You decided against that," Wright said.

"Maybe that was a mistake."

"Please!" said Merle.

They all climbed out of the car, stiff-legged, rumpled, and walked beneath the tree. The chief, wearing his poplin jacket but no longer the Magnum, instead carrying a small concealed revolver, looked like a member of a Fish and Game Club. Wright was in shirtsleeves. Merle stopped.

"I feel closer to Paula now than when she was alive." She peered at her husband. "Do you feel that way?"

Wright hooked an arm around her.

The chief was already at the door. He thumbed a button he suspected didn't work and then knocked on the door. The Wrights came up behind him, Merle composed, Wright poker-faced. The chief banged on the door and said, "I don't think she's home."

"What time is it?" Merle asked.

The chief raised his wrist. "Ten of four, but figure I'm five fast. Let's get something to eat. We'll come back."

"No," said Wright.

The chief shrugged and said, "I'll take a look around." He wandered around the side of the house, gazing at the ground for evidence of a small grave. The Wrights stayed near the door, Wright trying the bell again and listening for it, Merle working her weight from one leg to the other, while someone scrutinized them from the sidewalk.

The woman's face was flushed from walking, the underarms of her dress looped with stains, her bare arms bruised by a sun that didn't seem bright enough to do damage. She appeared unsure whether to advance or retreat. Then, as if forced, a small smile emerged. Her heated face turned tidy, and she stepped toward the house. Merle saw her first.

Merle squeezed Wright's arm. The tiny intense smile on the woman's face was undermined by eyes that seemed blinded for the moment.

"Are you waiting for me?" the woman asked. "I've been visiting a dear friend."

"Mrs. Leszkiewicz?" Merle asked, properly pronouncing the name. The chief appeared from around the side of the house and stopped short.

"Yes," said the woman pleasantly, wiping the perspiration from her nose. Her smile became a guilty grin. "I should have gone to work today, but I just didn't feel like it."

"Do you know who we are?" Merle asked, trying to steady her voice above her heavy heartbeat and looking the woman carefully in the eye.

"Yes, I think so."

"Where's my baby?" Merle screamed.

19

John Wright stayed at the door with his wife, while Chief Tull escorted May Leszkiewicz into her house. "I'm all right," Merle said, "and I'm not going to cry. I've done enough of that." They slipped into the house, Wright silently closing the door behind them.

"In here," the chief called from the kitchen. They passed through the living room, past a couch with bed clothes on it, slippers on the carpet, past an old floor-model television set with its little door flung back, like a store always open for business. The chief gestured, and they joined him at the table, where glasses had been set out. Mrs. Leszkiewicz was busy near the sink unscrewing a jar of Lipton's Ice Tea Mix.

"Nothing for us," Merle said.

"Oh, please, let me," she said, not turning around, reaching for a pitcher, running water. Merle heard her crack apart a plastic tray of ice cubes.

"I'm sorry I screamed at you," Merle said, and Mrs. Leszkiewicz looked over her shoulder. She had tears in her eyes, and Merle wondered how she could see through them.

"I understand," she said and busied herself again, her movements swift and sure, as if she enjoyed what she was doing, but when she carried the pitcher to the table her hand was trembling, partly because the pitcher was heavy. She poured ice tea into the glasses. One of the cubes fell into Merle's and splashed.

"Do you mind if we smoke?" Wright asked.

"No, I don't mind," she said. "Walter stopped smoking years ago, but let me see if I can find an ashtray." She returned with a saucer. "Will this do?"

"That's fine."

"Please sit with us," the chief said, and she sat down diffidently in the remaining chair like a waitress invited to join customers. Her eyes were drying. The chief said, "We heard about your husband's accident."

"People have been kind to me," she said, touching her glass of ice tea. "Please try yours," she said brightly to Merle. "It's good."

Merle did not move.

Mrs. Leszkiewicz said, "You remind me of somebody, somebody in the movies."

"Tell us about Patty," Wright said, and the chief scowled, a signal to Wright to take it slower. Mrs. Leszkiewicz glanced warmly at the chief, as though he were her friend. Wright said, "We knew her as Paula."

"Yes," she said, "I can see that. Her father's name, I think, was Paul."

Merle's breath caught. Wright said, "Her father is dead?"

"Oh, yes. Ages ago. I never knew him. He died the way Walter did, except Walter wasn't a drinker, and I guess that man was, from what I heard. He was a professor of something out there in Amherst, University of Massachusetts. That's where his accident was, out that way."

The chief, confused, said, "You aren't the mother?"

"Oh, no." She gave him a kindly look. "Walter and I

couldn't have children. That's one of the reasons we took Patty in. We got her from Family Services when she was six, starting first grade, though she could've gone right into second or third, she was so smart. This was her foster home. You people aren't drinking your ice tea." She took a large noisy swallow of her own, as if to encourage them.

"How long did she live here?" Wright said, anticipating her answer. She glanced at the chief, perhaps for guidance, and he seemed to nod.

"Till she was thirteen."

"Why did she leave?" Wright asked. The sun burst through the hazy sky and penetrated the kitchen, dust visible in its rays. Wright repeated the question.

"She ran away," Mrs. Leszkiewicz said softly.

"Did you look for her? Did you tell anybody?"

She did not reply.

"Does that mean you didn't?"

She looked at Wright but did not speak, and when the chief stirred she avoided his eyes. She swallowed more tea. Her face reminded Wright of the cold hard roll he had buttered for breakfast that morning.

He said, "People at Family Services must've known."

"No," she said, wiping her lips. "They were supposed to visit from time to time, but they never did except that once before we got her. And afterwards they only talked to me on the phone, when they happened to think about it."

"And you never told them," Wright said.

"No."

"For God's sake, why not?" Merle interjected, nearly knocking over the glass she hadn't touched.

"Please don't shout at me."

"I'm sorry," said Merle as the chief gestured.

The chief said, "Ma'am, why did Patty run away?"

"I don't know," Mrs. Leszkiewicz said in a drifting voice and stared into space, a hand dropping into her lap. "I was good to her. I washed her clothes, and I did up her dresses real nice for school."

"Mrs. Leskywick, look at me. You knew somebody killed her, didn't you? Did your husband tell you?"

"Oh, no," she said and gazed directly into the chief's eyes. "I saw that picture somebody drew in the paper. It didn't look much like her, not like I remembered her, but I knew it was her all the same."

"Did you and your husband talk about it?"

She glanced away again. "Maybe once or twice."

"That's all?"

"Yes. Don't shout."

"Mrs. Leskywick, I didn't shout. I didn't shout one bit."

She began to cry.

"Don't do that, ma'am," the chief said and shoved his chair closer to hers. Merle produced a tissue from her bag for him to give to her.

"Thank you," she said, dabbing her eyes. "I'm sorry. That's not like me."

"It's OK. You've been through a lot." The chief patted her shoulder. "But so have these people, and you know why they're here, don't you?"

"I guess so."

"OK, we know what we're doing now," he said, wrenching around in his chair to better look at her, and she smiled as if willing now to divulge secrets, confess sins. He said, "So I'm going to ask you again: why did the girl run away?"

She touched her hair, smoothed the back of it, and said, "She had to. She didn't have any choice."

"What do you mean?"

"She told me what was going on."

"Told you what?" said the chief impatiently. John and Merle Wright were immobile.

"She told me what he was doing with her."

"Your husband?"

"Yes, but he wouldn't have done it if she hadn't led him on in ways."

Merle, reaching for a tissue for herself now, said, "You don't believe that, do you?"

"Yes, I do!"

The two women fixed their gazes on each other. Mrs. Leszkiewicz lifted her chin, and Merle, crossing her long slim arms, said, "Then why did she bother to run away?"

"Because I told her to." Mrs. Leszkiewicz's voice was bold, her tone righteous. "I told her it was the only thing she could do. I wouldn't let her stay and break up my home. What would you have done? You tell me!"

The chief signaled Merle to say nothing. He had to signal twice, and then he coughed, priming himself. "Ma'am, let's talk about your husband."

She smiled lamely, her show of strength over. When she spoke her gaze was downward, and her voice fell. "Walter wasn't the same after that. He . . ."

The chief couldn't hear her, but it didn't matter. He had another question ready. "Ma'am, did he kill her?" He expected to horrify her, but he seemed merely to distract her. She drew in her shoulders, as if something cold had blown upon her.

"I don't know."

"Ma'am, be truthful. That's a question you've asked yourself, isn't it?"

"I don't know," she said faintly.

The chief's voice turned stern. "Yes, you do know. Now be honest with me."

Her eyes rolled back. "He could have, I don't know. Or it could've been her."

"Her?" the chief said, startled, glancing at the Wrights.

"I never liked her. I don't know why I called her."

"Called who?" said Wright, snapping forward.

"Patty's mother."

For a moment nobody reacted. Then Merle said, "You mean her mother's alive. She wasn't killed in the accident you told us about?"

"I never said she was," Mrs. Leszkiewicz said with a note of triumph. "She wasn't even in the car."

It was growing dark now, and they heard the large tree outside the house squeak like machinery in need of oiling. Moments later they heard the roar of two cars and the squeal of brakes from one of them, and Mrs. Leszkiewicz, interrupting herself, said, "Just boys." Then she smiled. "Where was I?"

"The hospital," the chief said.

"Not the hospital I work at, but the mental one."

"Yes, we understand that."

She went on, wound up, her voice at times a smooth rush and other times erratic, out of tune, jumping keys. She wiped her hair back, her face moist, her dress wilting on her body, as Wright sat with an unlighted cigarette in his hand. Merle sat in a shadow, her eyes like holes. Only the chief was hunched forward, with both elbows on the table.

"It's only ten minutes from here, on a hill. You could go there, see for yourself. It's not a bad place, not what you'd expect."

"Wait," said the chief. "What I don't understand is if she's still there, locked up. You're talking like she is."

"Oh, no. She was in and out, but sometimes she was in for long periods. Am I making sense now?"

"You just take it slow," he said. She smiled and reached for the pitcher, but he took it from her. "Let me do it," he said and refilled her glass. The ice cubes had long ago melted.

Mrs. Leszkiewicz drank heartily, wiped her mouth, and said sardonically, "Miss Amherst, that's what she thought she still was, some beauty queen, if she ever really was. My husband said she probably got the title from all the boys who—well, I won't repeat what he said."

"Did she go to Amherst College?" Merle asked.

Mrs. Leszkiewicz looked toward the shadow and seemed to sneer into it. "She went the same place her husband did his teaching, University of Massachusetts, but maybe she thought the other school was fancier and wanted people to think that's where she went. That's what my husband said. He said she put on airs anybody could see through."

The chief, taking notes now in the half-light, said, "Was she a student when she married her husband? Ahouse you said his name was."

Mrs. Leszkiewicz took time to pull her dress away from her shoulders where it was sticking. Her breathing was labored, yet she looked happy, as if she were sharing mild gossip with nice folks, as she often did with patients at the hospital, those who were awake, those who would listen or had no choice. The chief's ballpoint pen remained ready.

"Ma'am?"

"Ahouse, yes. What was your question?"

"Was she a student when—"

"She must've been. He was older, I heard, and she

started tricking him right from the start and worse after little Patty was born, like she was mad at him for giving her a baby, I mean if you believe it was his. My husband said she drove him to drink the same way she drove him to his accident, just as if she was sitting next to him and pushing at the wheel."

"Your husband seemed to know her pretty well."

"The social worker that brought Patty told us stuff, and Walter said he didn't have to know her to *know* her, just looking at her was enough, the way she dressed and all, like she was still Miss Amherst."

"She came to this house?"

"Sure she did," Mrs. Leszkiewicz said, putting a hand to her breast to catch her breath. "When she'd get out of the hospital, she'd come straight here, even though a court order said she couldn't. And Patty didn't want to see her and used to hide. I never saw a child so scared. That woman was good at pretending. She'd hug Patty and do it too hard, enough to make her cry and then some, like paying her back."

Merle abruptly materialized out of the shadow. "Paying her back for what?"

Mrs. Leszkiewicz pulled back in her chair, resenting Merle's intrusion, obviously comfortable only when the chief spoke. He said gently, "We're stirring up a lot of bad memories, I bet."

She nodded, grateful for his understanding.

"You want to wash your face or something?" he asked.

She nodded again, warmed that he should understand even that need. They watched her shuffle out of the kitchen and heard her climb the stairs, close a door, use the toilet.

The chief said, "We've got to take it slow with her."

"We're taking it too slow," Merle said.

"Keep your voices down," Wright said. "You can hear everything in this house."

She came back with her hair brushed and a little color on her lips and some on her cheeks. The chief rose and signaled Wright to do the same, and the two of them stood like soldiers for a war widow. She seemed refreshed in one way but deeply fatigued in another, perspiring more than before, her dress clinging wetly to her.

"There," said the chief, resuming his place, flexing a leg. Mrs. Leszkiewicz smiled mysteriously at everybody, her expression girlish. The chief said, "What I can't figure out is why Patty's mother acted that way toward her. Doesn't seem natural."

Mrs. Leszkiewicz tilted her head. "She was that kind of woman."

"What kind, ma'am? Tell us."

She fidgeted. "I wish Walter was here. He could tell you better. He saw her good."

"Tell us what you saw, ma'am."

"She whispered things in Patty's ear and showed her those ugly scars, like Patty was to blame."

"What scars?" said Merle.

"Shhhh," said the chief.

Mrs. Leszkiewicz wheezed. "She acted like Patty was to blame for everything because of the judge."

"What judge?" Merle demanded, and Mrs. Leszkiewicz put a protective hand to her breast.

"The judge took Patty and asked her questions about her mother. Patty wasn't but five, and she didn't want to tell, but the judge said they were only trying to help her mommy. The social worker told us how the judge put Patty right on his knee and got her to talk. Anyway that's when Miss Amherst went to the hospital the first time."

Merle was immobile, her face bloodless. Mrs. Leszkiewicz began to sob.

"I loved Patty," she said. "Don't you know that?"

Merle stared at her and said, "No, I don't know that."

The chief clicked his ballpoint as Mrs. Leszkiewicz swayed in her chair. He started to reach out to her but jerked his hand back. Her dress had come unfastened in back, revealing a sponge of flesh that reminded him of the mushroom he had seen in the state forest. She turned deliberately toward him, her eyes hot and bitter.

"I don't want those two sitting at my table anymore," she said.

Outside in the purpling dark, under the tree, Merle said, "I don't trust her. I don't even know if I believe her." Wright wrapped an arm around her because she had the chills and couldn't shake them. They heard the quick twitter of a bird from a high branch, then the twitching of leaves as the bird flew away.

"I believe her," the chief said, and then qualified it. "At least I think I do."

Merle shivered.

"Here," said the chief, stripping off his poplin. "You put this over your shoulders. Go ahead."

Wright helped her with it, and she tightened it about her throat. The chief stood out larger than life in his stiff white police shirt, the badge glaring from the breast pocket. Merle said, "God, I've got to use a bathroom."

"Go around the side of the house," the chief suggested. "Bushes back there."

Merle stole away.

The chief dangled his arms clenching and unclenching his fists, as if he felt events were getting away from him. He said to Wright, "When she comes back, why don't you two wait in the car. I want to talk to that woman a bit more."

Wright gave him no argument, and he strode back to the door, rapped once, and entered the dim of the house. He called her name, but she neither heard nor saw him, and for moments he failed to see her. Then, in the depths of the living room, he glimpsed the drift of her shape in the grayness. She was wrapped in a robe.

"Oh," she said, startled. "I was just about to take my bath."

"Sorry," he said, ill at ease.

She wavered between cracks of lights emanating from the kitchen and then drifted toward him with the hint of a smile. The chief stood rocked forward.

"You took your jacket off," she said with pleasant surprise, as if perhaps he had come back to stay. He rearranged his stance, and her eyes dropped to his belt. "What's that?" she asked, mildly disconcerted.

"Revolver."

"Oh."

She seemed giddy, and he wanted to shake her but feared putting a hand on her. Her robe was tightly wrapped around her, the small collar raised. She smiled with vague anxiety.

"I'm a policeman. You knew that."

"No, you didn't say."

"Yes, I did, ma'am. Right at the very beginning I did, even before they came into the house."

"Thank you for making them go."

"Let's sit down," he said and moved toward a chair, stepping over a dress, underclothes, and stumbling on a shoe. She switched on a weak light that would have been impossible to read by and sat near him on a hassock, keeping her robe together with both hands, one naked foot curled over the other, the toes dug in.

"Ma'am, your husband went looking for Patty, didn't he?"

Her voice swam toward him with sudden bitterness: "He never stopped looking for her. I knew all these years he was doing that, why he lost his job and all and didn't look for another."

"And he finally found her, didn't he?"

She looked away. "I don't know for sure."

"Ma'am, if he did kill Patty, what would he have done with the little girl? I don't imagine she's still alive, do you? Where would he have put the body?"

She gave him a haggard look. "You keep talking about him. Why don't you talk about her?"

"Patty's mother?"

"She *knew*."

The chief cocked his head. "What did she know?"

"She knew why Patty ran away just by looking at us, like it was written on our faces. She knew everything, I could tell, but she treated me like I didn't matter, and she said something like *you poor bastard* to Walter, like maybe she had a little feeling for him but none for me, and acting like she was glad it happened because it showed I didn't give Patty proper care, which was a lie. I did!"

She reeled on the hassock, while clutching her robe, knotting the material. The chief rubbed his eyes in a way that caught her attention, and she flinched, as if touched by a dead hand. Wearily the chief said, "I guess that's really why I came back. It's her I guess I've got to talk to."

"Yes. Leave Walter alone!"

She rose unsteadily on stout legs, and the chief rose too, with a jolt, prepared to steady her.

"Walter's dead," she said. "You can't hurt him. Hurt her!"

"Ma'am, I don't want to hurt anybody. And I certainly don't want to hurt you."

Her eyes welled with tears.

"Ma'am, do you know where I might find her?"

"You get a Boston phone book," she said, her voice deepening, as if she were speaking for her husband. "That'll tell you. And if it don't, you call the telephone company. Irene Ahouse. You got that?"

"Yes, ma'am," he said, patting a pocket. "I've got it written down."

She tottered.

"Ma'am, you going to be all right?"

"Oh yes," she said, taking a stumbling step. He darted to her, and she reacted to the white flash of his shirt. He placed calming hands on her. Her robe was loose now, her body like an open oven. He felt the heat in his hands, and he felt something else, some change. He leaned back. "I'm going to be fine," she whispered. "I might go to Florida. That's what I might do."

"That sounds nice," the chief said, slowly releasing her.

"Oh yes. That's what Walter would've wanted."

She was no longer looking at him directly, and her face seemed folded, nothing more to say. Feeling something fragile for her, he bent forward and gave her a fast awkward kiss on her crumpled cheek.

"You go take your bath now," he said.

They drove into the billowing darkness of Route 2, one headlight paving the way and Wright telling himself he should have got the other fixed by now. Merle's hands were clasped in her lap. The chief, blocking a yawn, picked up where he had left off, his voice a drone, sometimes inaudible. Great chunks of light bore down on them, giant trucks passing at high speeds into the gentle threat of rain, no drivers visible, as if the trucks ran by remote control triggered thousands of miles away. The first drops were nicks on the windshield, and Wright waited for more before working the wipers. The chief, interrupting himself, said, "If it didn't rain that other night, we'd of had her husband."

"No," said Merle. "It didn't rain in Ballardville. He went looking for it."

20

The young waiter, wearing a turtleneck jersey under a peach-colored sports jacket, smoked his cigarette down to the filter and snapped it at pigeons waiting for peanuts. The Common was crowded, and he was sharing a bench with an elderly woman reading the Christian Science *Monitor*. He alternately looked at his watch and at his white shoes.

"Nicholas, how are you? It's good to see you."

The voice, which yanked him to his feet, belonged to a short man with brushed-back graying hair, a shiny brow, heavy glasses and a thick nose.

"It's good to see you, sir."

"Been waiting long?"

"No, sir."

"Let's walk."

Nicholas adjusted his long stride to the man's short one. They walked under a tree, a squirrel watching them. They walked into the sun toward another tree.

"How's your mother?" the man asked. "She OK?"

"She's doing good," Nicholas said. "I'll tell her you asked."

"Tell her I shoulda married her. My wife don't make lasagna good as her."

"I'll tell her that. She'll get a kick out of it."

They stopped in the shade. The man said, "How's your boss? I haven't seen him lately."

"Well, you know he's got a lot on his mind. He's got problems, I guess you heard."

The man flashed his teeth. "He got too much heart, that's his biggest problem. Him and his sister taking in a girl like that, that wasn't even Italian. It was bound to turn out bad. Hard to understand why he did it."

"The Feds are using that," Nicholas said. "Otherwise I think they'd have stopped bothering us by now."

"That's for sure," the man said. "Puts him in a spot."

Nicholas nodded.

"He worries us," the man said.

Nicholas nodded again, lips glued together.

"He don't listen to us. That worries us the most."

Nicholas looked the man in the eye. "I'm available for whatever you want, you know that."

The man smoothed his hair back. "No, nothing like that, Nicholas. But we think it'd be good all round if he went away awhile on something little. In cases like this, a little time in the can is good for the soul, long as you know it's not forever."

"Right," said Nicholas.

" 'Course it hurts us to do it. We love that man."

"I know what you mean," Nicholas said. "I love him like a father."

The man smiled. "Sure you do, Nicholas. What I wanted to see you about is, can you handle his place while he's away? I mean, *everything*. You be like a manager for him while he has his rest."

Nicholas's eyes brightened, but his voice stayed casual. "Sure, I could handle it. No problem."

"Good boy," the man said and slapped Nicholas's shoulder. "You do a good job, who knows, maybe when he comes back he'll want to retire, go live in Saugus or somewhere."

"Thank you for the opportunity you're giving me."

"How old are you now, Nicholas?"

"Twenty-five."

"Yeah, you ought to thank me."

They began to walk again, the man with an eye on Nicholas's peach jacket. He reached out and touched the sleeve, felt the material.

"Where'd you learn to dress like that? You pick it up yourself?"

"This is part of a special shipment fell into my hands."

"You're a hot shit, Nicholas."

Cogger placed a napkin and a Styrofoam cup of coffee on Spence's desk and peeled the cap off. The coffee was black and too hot to drink yet. Spence said, "Didn't you get one for yourself?"

"No," said Cogger. "I've been drinking too much lately, stomach's upset."

"Sit down," Spence said and made his mouth round for a moment. "What do you think of that chief, not keeping in touch, not calling?"

"Maybe it just got too much for him, and he took a day off and went fishing."

Spence scoffed. "He wouldn't know how to bait a hook."

Cogger crossed his legs. His face was drawn.

Spence said, "Maybe you should go fishing. You don't look so well. What's the matter?"

"Just a little tired."

"You have a vacation coming up, haven't you?"

"No rush."

Spence reached for his coffee and sipped it cautiously. He said, "I've been thinking, maybe we can spare a man. Let's put him on the chief. Maybe you could even handle it yourself."

Chief Tull, sitting in a window booth in the luncheonette, forsook his usual cruller and ate three dropped eggs on toast and two glasses of grapefruit juice. Still hungry, he ordered a bag of potato chips and another glass of juice, and the waitress said, "Boy, I haven't seen you eat like this in a long time."

The chief said nothing. His eating was of the nervous kind. Munching chips, he watched people crisscrossing the street against mild traffic. He saw the spry step of a man in a see-through summer shirt, a real estate agent who had almost sold him a new house when he had made chief, but the bank had wanted too much money down. He remembered the house had had a nice yard, apple trees in back and along one side, and a laundry room that had appealed to his wife. Finishing the chips and crunching up the bag, he spotted a youth who looked a little like the Oliver boy and maybe was. Quickly he turned his head, experiencing a burning in his stomach, a need to break wind, an anger at himself. When he looked back, he saw the Wrights.

They sat with him. Wright laid his package of Kents on the table and ordered two coffees, and Merle pushed the hair from her face. Both looked as though they had not slept. The chief repositioned the salt and pepper shakers, edged out the ashtray, played with packets of sugar and then distributed a few on the table for use. When the waitress brought the coffees, she said insinuatingly, "Anything more for you, Chief?"

He dismissed her with a wave and watched Merle cream her coffee. There were a few stray strands of gray in her hair that he was sure had not been there before. Wright lit two cigarettes and passed one to Merle, and the chief tried to remember the movie that had popularized that gesture. "I think I'll have one of those," he said and reached for the package. Wright lit it for him. They smoked in silence for a while.

"We don't have to go to the telephone company," the chief said, tapping loose an ash. "She's not hiding."

Merle nodded. "For some reason, I didn't think she would be."

"Phone book says Revere Street. You know where that is?"

"Beacon Hill," Wright said. "The side that isn't so nice anymore. We used to live around there."

The chief tried to smooth out the potato chip bag he had crumpled. "There's something I'd like to ask you people," he said, his eyes on his work.

"Go ahead," said Wright.

"This will probably be the last place, the end of the line. What happens if your daughter's not there?"

Wright sat back as Merle stirred her coffee. He said, "We'll keep on looking."

The chief sucked on his cigarette.

Wright said, "What the hell else can we do?"

The chief put the cigarette out. "Do you want to use your car again?"

"It got us to Gardner," said Wright. "I think it'll take us to Boston and back."

21

The sun was milky and Beacon Hill steamy from the promise of too much heat and the inescapable odor of dog droppings on cobble and brick. Steep and tilted, the streets were no more than jagged openings between parked cars, as bad as in the North End and in some spots more treacherous. Wright, ascending the Hill from the Cambridge Street side, maneuvered the Cutlass nearly to the top and then angled onto Revere Street, where the clutter of cars was greater, no chance of finding a parking space. Chief Tull hung an arm out and pointed to a doorway in a narrow brick building.

"That's it."

Wright nodded. "I know." And he kept on going as Merle looked back at it.

"Try Phillips," he said.

Phillips Street was parallel with Revere and had nothing to offer. The Cutlass slid gradually back to Cambridge Street and got caught in merciless traffic headed toward Government Center. The chief swabbed his heated face with his sleeve, while Wright, edging toward an outside lane, sought to reverse their direction.

"Park anywhere," Merle said. "We'll walk."

Wright reversed directions twice and finally found a space at the foot of Cambridge, between a gas station and a bar called the Harvard Gardens. The Wrights were out of the car before the chief, who called them back.

"Better lock up," he said, coughing, too many exhaust fumes around him, his hand beating the air.

They began to hike the Hill, single file, heavy going up a narrow sidewalk tilted inward and fouled by animals. Wright was in the lead, and the chief carried the rear, puffing, mopping his forehead and glancing into windows of basement apartments. The pace was too much for him, and he fell behind.

"No so fast," he said, stumbling and stepping where he shouldn't have. "Oh, Christ!"

The Wrights waited while he scraped his shoe, caught his breath, shrugged off his poplin. Wright's face was tense and Merle agitated, her teeth showing, her slim shoulders set. People edged by them, staring at the chief, who smiled curiously at them. He felt tired and dull all over. He looked at the Wrights with the same odd smile.

"I've got lead in my legs."

Merle came to him, and he met her eyes, which perhaps he was truly doing for the first time. He thought of some small things he might like to say to her at another time. Her hand passed over his forehead.

"Are you all right?"

"Little dizzy. You people go on. I'll catch up. You can talk to her and kind of feel her out until I get there."

"Chief, are you sure?"

"Yes."

Wright stepped toward him with the keys to the Cutlass. "Here. In case you want to go back and sit down."

The chief scoffed.

"Take them anyway."

Perched in place with a shoulder against brick, he watched the Wrights make the climb until he could no longer see them, other people in the way. A hot gust of exhaust from a rattling taxi had both a sickly and soporific effect on him, and he wavered against the wall of the building, glancing down at a window and glimpsing books on a table and a candle in a wine bottle. Pushing a hand over his wet face and hair, he realized he could not remain where he was. The sun was stewing him.

He was halfway back to the Cutlass before he was aware of his steps, as if his body had acted automatically, no longer bothering to consult him. A poodle appeared out of a doorway, straining at its leash and yapping at him. He steadied himself and poised a foot, daring the dog to come near, but the little animal was wary, maybe even smart, and instantly obeyed its owner's tug on the leash.

Sitting in the Cutlass, windows lowered, the chief considered the curious heaviness in his chest and stomach and down into his legs, even his toes, and waited for it to pass. He stared dreamily at traffic on Cambridge Street, as if each passing car were a reflection in a faraway mirror. He heard sounds from the service station and caught the smell of gasoline, pleasant only for a moment. Stronger was the odor of what he had stepped in, some of it obviously still on his shoes, which he had spit-polished that morning. He thought of the Oliver boy and the anonymous gift of money he was planning to send him. What made him think of that was the bank across the street, the Boston Five, for he would need a loan, the amount not yet determined. As he toyed with figures, a pain sprouted in his chest.

He had a damned good idea what was happening

and wasn't frightened. For one thing, he had been through this with others, his own father in fact, who was still alive; and for another, Mass General lay just beyond the Boston Five. The fear came when he realized that his voice, which he had thought quite bold, was attracting nobody. He angled an arm toward the horn but couldn't reach it, couldn't even come close, and his hand dropped uselessly to the seat as if it had fallen a great distance. A breeze wafted into the Cutlass, and he felt his thin hair wisping.

A door opened at the Harvard Gardens, and a young woman came out, as slender and dark-haired as Merle Wright. He closed his eyes and for a moment felt the fragile weight of Merle Wright's breast upon his arm as she cooled his forehead with her hand. He imagined the soft musky scent of her underarm as she spoke to him. Licking his lips, he tasted ginger ale. He opened his eyes and saw the young woman approaching the car, her stride carefree.

His voice was useless, so he smiled.

The door opened into a hallway painted a harsh blue, as if to hide dirt. Only some of the mailboxes had names. An old man, elfin, scarcely five feet, appeared at the stair-bottom and said, "Who you looking for?"

"Mrs. Ahouse," Wright said.

"I forget names. What does she look like?"

Merle stepped forward. "Probably a little over forty, probably blond."

The old man scratched his head. His gray hair looked like ash ready to blow away. "Must be the one on the third floor, number nine. You can try it."

Merle stepped closer. "Do you know whether she has a child? A little girl, sixteen months old now."

He shook his head. "Don't know of any little girl here, but I think I've seen somebody with a little boy. She might be the one."

The banister on the second landing was unsteady and shook under their grip. Number nine was to the left. Wright exchanged a look with his wife before knocking. No one answered, and he knocked a little harder.

"Try it," said Merle.

He twisted the knob, and the door sprang open. He looked into a room that smelled mildly of incense and strongly of cigarette smoke, with an arty calendar and Chagall prints on the white walls. He stepped in. "Hello. Mrs. Ahouse."

Someone moved as Wright took another step inside, Merle close behind him and then suddenly beside him.

A man who had been partially obscured was now visible. He was middle-aged but dressed to look young, with sprayed hair and tight pants. He reached for his sports jacket, and giving it a quick brush, said, "I'm just a visitor, just leaving."

Wright started to speak and stopped. A woman wearing shorts came out of a bedroom, closed the door behind her and stood with a hand on her hip, her long thighs so white they looked chalked.

"Irene, I'll catch you later," the man said, hurriedly, on his way out.

She paid no attention to him, her eyes on the Wrights, their eyes on her. She was tall and had hair the color of twine and a handsome face despite rough surfaces, sharp edges, and a nose dented as though by a long-ago blow. She wore an opaque blouse over a bra that gave her thrusting breasts.

"Who the hell are you two?"

"I'm John Wright. This is my wife, Merle."

"Well, that's nice, whoever the hell you still are. What are you doing in my place?"

Before Wright could answer, she gestured with two stiff fingers near her mouth. She wanted a cigarette. Wright walked to her and gave her one. Scars were visible on her wrist, some dark, the color of iodine. He met her eyes, blank and pitiless one instant, almost pleasant the next. Her scent was oversweet. He stepped back.

Merle said, "I understand you have a little boy."

The woman inhaled a great deal of smoke and exhaled it slowly. "That so? Who told you that?"

"Do you?"

"You out of your mind?" She laughed, the joke on her, not altogether funny. "That's a stupid question, right, honey? If you were out of your mind, how could you give me a rational answer?"

"I'd find a way," Merle said.

"Wow. Pretty quick on your feet, honey. Who do you practice on, him?" Her eyes raced to Wright. "I bet she's a ball-breaker. Is she?"

"Mrs. Ahouse," Wright said, and she took a fast drag on the cigarette, an ash hurtling to the floor.

"What can I do for you? Sit down, though I don't know why in hell you're here. Either of you want a beer? I've got the light stuff for you, Miss Trim. Just say the word."

"No thank you," Merle said.

The woman snubbed out the cigarette in a potted plant. Then she snapped her fingers. "Say, I've got it. I put an ad in the *Phoenix,* three's company sort of thing, and you people are answering it. Hey, great!"

The Wrights said nothing.

"Hey, I'm only kidding, for Christ's sake." Her smile turned grim. "You two are something. You don't want a beer, and you don't want to sit down. Let's see, do you know the way out?"

Wright, strangely free of tension, said, "You know who we are, don't you?"

"Honey, I'm not psychic. I'm a lot of things, mind you, but not that."

"We were in Gardner," he said. "Mrs. Leszkiewicz told us about you."

The woman seemed to rise up and then, as if to bring herself down, dug her hands into the tight front pockets of her shorts, straining the material, nearly popping the fly zipper. She smiled. "A dear sweet lady. I always wondered what her cranial measurements were. I think the sweetheart's got her problems, don't you?"

"Do you mind if we talk about it?"

"Do you mind if I ask you something? What the hell is this, a grand inquisition?"

"Call it what you like," Wright said, and the woman laughed.

"Hey, I like you. I think you two go together. Honest." She scratched a thigh. "I don't mind questions. Who do you want to talk about, the hound dog? I hear he's dead."

"Hound dog?"

"Walter! Who else? A horny bastard with all the instincts of a hunter."

A hand flew out of her pocket. She wanted another cigarette, and Wright moved instantly and again lighted it for her. He stayed where he was, taking the smoke in the face and watching her mouth twist into a glistening rose muscle.

"That fucking old man," she said, just loud enough to be heard.

Merle stepped forward, and the woman shifted hard to one side, not wanting to be hemmed in. She held her cigarette high, as if ready to fling it. The scars on her raised wrist reminded Merle of little sea creatures.

"Look, I know who you are, I knew as soon as I saw you, but there're certain things I don't want to talk about. Understand?"

"Some things we must talk about," Merle said.

The woman stared at her almost with amusement, studying her hair, her eyes. "You must hate me."

"I have no time for that," Merle said, feeling herself go cold, a terrible chill.

"Don't blame me, honey. Blame him. That degenerate hunted poor Patty down. It was him she was scared of, not me. Him that kept her on the run. I was doing OK not knowing where she was. Hell, I didn't even *want* to know, but he had to find me and tell me, like he was expecting me to give him a prize."

Merle was shaking her head.

"What's the matter, honey? I lose you somewhere?"

"He didn't like you. Why would he tell you anything?"

"Honey, don't try to figure out a guy like that. He never played with a full deck in his life, know what I mean?"

The woman gave Merle a tight smile.

"I don't want to scare you, honey, but you look like you could use some help yourself."

Merle's throat was too dry for her to speak. Wright said, "Your daughter was frightened of him, but she was just as scared of you."

The woman didn't answer, her eyes on Merle, who

was edging away, and craning her neck to peer into the small kitchen. A box of Boo Berry cereal on the table.

"What are you looking at, Big Eyes?"

Merle forced a smile. She said, "You *do* have a child here. May I see him?"

The woman ground her cigarette out in the pot. "He's having his nappy-nap, OK? Hasn't been feeling well lately, a bit of an ear infection."

Merle felt her body quake. "Please let me see him."

Before the woman could stop her, Merle pushed past her, flung open the bedroom door and saw Marcie.

Marcie lay asleep on a big bed in a boy's polo shirt and overalls, her dark hair chopped, her face flushed from an inflamed ear and a temperature. She woke with a hovering parent on each side of her and stared at them wide-eyed, her face tightening, her small mouth quivering, as if too many thoughts were hatching all at once in her hot head.

"Darling, it's mommy," Merle said, sobbing.

The child stared at her as if she did not remember her, or remembered her but no longer trusted her.

"Sweetheart, don't you know me?"

The child began to cry, and Merle gathered her up and stood rocking her, as Wright embraced them both. The woman stood in the doorway peering into the shade-drawn room. She appeared set to leave, a heavy shoulder bag hanging from her left side.

"I suppose you want her back," she said in a dull voice. Then she smiled at Marcie, caught her eye, and said, "Patty, you want to go with these people or you want to stay with mama?"

"Her name is Marcie!" Merle said.

The woman stiffened. "Don't tell me what the fuck her name is. I know what her name is. What's your name, honey. Tell these sweet people."

Marcie was shaking, still wide-eyed, half hugging one woman while anticipating the grasp of another. She freed a hand to fuss with her aching ear, and the woman's eyes softened.

"Mama got you medicine for that, didn't she?"

Wright said, "This is our daughter, Marcie. Your daughter was Patty."

"What do you mean, *was*. Who the hell are you?"

"We knew her. She called herself Paula."

The woman swayed against the door jamb. "Oh yeah. That was some night. Jesus!" She made the gesture for a cigarette. Wright tossed her the pack.

"Keep them, Mrs. Ahouse."

"Call me Irene. Lots do." She searched her bag for a match, found a book of them and lit the cigarette with a shaky hand. "I haven't seen the kid in years, and she looks at me like I'm something out of a horror movie. Doesn't want me to touch her, like I got shit on my fingers or something. I'm her mother, for Christ's sake. I want to look at my kid, see how she's developed, and she tells me to get out, leave her alone. The miserable little snot!"

"You didn't need to hit her," Wright said quietly. With her eyes, Merle measured the distance to the door.

"So I gave her a hit. You never hit anybody?"

"You didn't just hit her once. You hit her quite a few times, and I think you know with what.'"

The woman put a hand to her forehead, the one with the cigarette between the fingers. "Oh Christ, I didn't mean to. How is she?" Her hand flew down, spraying sparks. "No, don't tell me. I don't want to know."

"She's dead."

"I said I didn't want to know!"

Marcie began to cry again.

The woman stuck the cigarette in her mouth, reached into her bag and came out with a hammer. "You shut up!" She lunged not so much at Marcie as at Merle. It was Merle she was looking at.

Wright threw a punch.

Agent Cogger, watching from his car, which was double-parked, saw Chief Tull's head loll back and the young woman yank open the door of the Cutlass. In the next instant he was running toward them.

"What the hell's going on?" he said, grabbing at the woman, pulling her. "Leave him alone, will you!"

She twisted around, fighting him. "God-damn it, I'm a nurse."

"I don't give a damn who you are," he said, flashing identification. "Step back!"

He thrust his head into the Cutlass and did not like what he smelled, and then he did not like what he saw. The blotches on the chief's face were prickly, the lips purple. He withdrew slowly. The young woman glared at him.

"Is he still alive?" he asked meekly.

"I don't know. Get out of the way. Get an ambulance."

A crowd began to gather, and Cogger broke through it and began walking toward the gas station. "Holy shit," he muttered and whipped out a handkerchief to wipe his face. Then he stopped in his tracks.

Coming down a steep street were the Wrights, a child in Merle Wright's arms.

22

BOSTON (AP)—Federal agents and Boston police yesterday arrested a former mental patient for the May 5 murder of her 19-year-old daughter and the abduction of a child.

The FBI apprehended Irene Ahouse, 42, at her Revere Street apartment on Beacon Hill, where she was holding Marcie Wright, 16 months, daughter of John and Merle Wright of Ballardville. The child was taken to Massachusetts General Hospital for treatment of a severe ear infection and other maladies.

Ahouse, formerly of Amherst, was arraigned in Boston Municipal Court and charged with bludgeoning to death Patricia Ahouse (aka Paula Aherne) at the home of Mr. and Mrs. Wright, where the young woman was babysitting, and with kidnapping the child.

C. Ellison Spence, agent in charge of the investigation, said the arrest followed an arduous investigation that included tracing the murdered woman's identity, which she had "carefully con-

cealed for personal reasons, one being the fear of her mother.''

Spence said that a tragic footnote to the case was the death of Ballardville Police Chief Edmund Tull, 51, who was on hand for the arrest but was stricken with a coronary thrombosis shortly before authorities swooped down on the Revere Street dwelling.

Spence said Tull had contributed to the probe in a number of ways and...

A
psychopathic
killer
strikes without warning
and with no
apparent motive.

Experience chills and terror as the people involved struggle to discover why they are being stalked and who is responsible for these frightening occurrences. Follow the painstaking pursuit of the police as they rush to apprehend the killers, before they can strike again.

_____82315   **THE MAJORETTES**, John Russo $1.95

_____82233   **FIELDS OF EDEN**, Michael T. Hinkemeyer $1.95

_____82326   **THE BAIT**, Dorothy Uhnak $1.95

_____82756   **LOVE KILLS**, Dan Greenburg $2.50

_____81247   **MICHIGAN MURDERS**, Edward Keyes $2.50

_____82871   **LOOKING FOR MR. GOODBAR**, Judith Rossner $2.75

POCKET BOOKS Department HOR
1230 Avenue of the Americas, New York, N.Y. 10020

Please send me the books I have checked above. I am enclosing $_____ (please add 50¢ to cover postage and handling for each order, N.Y.S. and N.Y.C. residents please add appropriate sales tax). Send check or money order—no cash or C.O.D.s please. Allow up to six weeks for delivery.

NAME_____

ADDRESS_____

CITY_____ STATE/ZIP_____

HOR 10-79

RIVETING MYSTERIES

Ingenious plots that will hold you spellbound to the very end. Page-turning action and plenty of suspense. Characters that live—and love—you'll never forget them.

Discerning readers everywhere are choosing these bestselling thrillers from Pocket Books:

_____ 80915   THE KEY TO MIDNIGHT Leigh Nichols $2.50

_____ 82678   THE GLENDOWER LEGACY Thomas Gifford $2.50

_____ 82384   A FAMILY FORTUNE Jerome Weidman $2.50

_____ 81735   THE HENDERSON EQUATION Warren Adler $2.25

_____ 82110   CIRCUS COURONNE R. Wright Campbell $2.25

_____ 82111   SPY WHO SAT AND WAITED R. Wright Campbell $2.50

_____ 82479   BOTTOM LINE Fletcher Knebel $2.50

_____ 80416   TRESPASS Fletcher Knebel $1.95

_____ 81988   TRUE CONFESSIONS John Gregory Dunne $2.50

- -

POCKET BOOKS
Department MYSa
1230 Avenue of the Americas
New York, N.Y. 10020

 **OCKET BOOKS**

Please send me the books I have checked above. I am enclosing $_____ (please add 50¢ to cover postage and handling for each order, N.Y.S. and N.Y.C. residents please add appropriate sales tax). Send check or money order—no cash or C.O.D.s please. Allow up to six weeks for delivery.

NAME_____

ADDRESS_____

CITY_____ STATE/ZIP_____

MYSa 6-79

The Terrifying Genius of
HERBERT LIEBERMAN

Critics rave:

CRAWLSPACE: *"A horror story from which there is no exit."* —Kirkus Reviews

THE EIGHTH SQUARE: *"Unique in suspense novels."* — San Francisco Chronicle

BRILLIANT KIDS: *"Fast-paced, always interesting."* —Business Week

CITY OF THE DEAD: *"Brutal, morbidly fascinating."* —Playboy

Readers tremble.
Send for these Herbert Lieberman novels of horror and suspense. From Pocket Books.

_____ 81411 BRILLIANT KIDS 1.95
_____ 80877 CITY OF THE DEAD 1.95
_____ 81455 CRAWLSPACE 1.95
_____ 81425 EIGHTH SQUARE 1.95
_____ 82236 CLIMATE OF HELL $2.50

POCKET BOOKS
Department HL
1230 Avenue of the Americas
New York, N.Y. 10020

Please send me the books I have checked above. I am enclosing $_____ (please add 50¢ to cover postage and handling for each order, N.Y.S. and N.Y.C. residents please add appropriate sales tax). Send check or money order—no cash or C.O.D.s please. Allow up to six weeks for delivery.

NAME_____

ADDRESS_____

CITY_____STATE/ZIP_____

HL 11-79

THE OCCULT:

events sometimes real, sometimes
imagined. Always haunting.
Psychological thrillers guaranteed to
keep readers in the grip of fear.
Chilling books—

available now from
POCKET BOOKS

_____ 81891	**INITIATION,**	
	Elizabeth Haich $2.50	
_____ 41051	**JULIA,** Peter Straub $2.75	
_____ 41052	**IF YOU COULD SEE ME NOW,**	
	Peter Straub $2.75	
_____ 82215	**DEVIL'S GAMBLE,**	
	Frank G. Slaughter $2.50	
_____ 82222	**SEA CLIFF,**	
	Michael T. Hinkemeyer $1.95	
_____ 81689	**LITTLE ANGIE,**	
	Emma Cave $1.95	
_____ 41014	**EDUCATION OF OVERSOUL**	
	#7, Jane Roberts $2.50	
_____ 81948	**DEMON SUMMER,**	
	Elaine Booth Selig $1.95	

POCKET BOOKS Department OCa
1230 Avenue of the Americas, New York, N.Y. 10020

Please send me the books I have checked above. I am enclosing $_____
(please add 50¢ to cover postage and handling for each order, N.Y.S. and N.Y.C.
residents please add appropriate sales tax). Send check or money order—no
cash or C.O.D.s please. Allow up to six weeks for delivery.

NAME_____

ADDRESS_____

CITY_____ STATE/ZIP_____

OCa 2-80

Bestselling Novels from #1 POCKET BOOKS

_____ 83649-8 THE CRASH OF '79, Paul Erdman $2.95

_____ 41153 FLOWERS IN THE ATTIC, V.C. Andrews $2.75

_____ 82388 GOOD AS GOLD, Joseph Heller $2.95

_____ 80915 THE KEY TO MIDNIGHT, Leigh Nichols $2.50

_____ 82801 LAUREL CANYON, Steve Krantz $2.50

_____ 82756 LOVE KILLS, Dan Greenburg $2.50

_____ 82938 NEW YORK, N.Y. 10022, Steve Kahn $2.50

_____ 82843 THE ROGUE, Janet Dailey $2.50

_____ 83531 WIFEY, Judy Blume $2.75

_____ 83312 THE WINDS OF WAR, Herman Wouk $3.50

_____ 83515 THE WORLD ACCORDING TO GARP, John Irving $3.50

POCKET BOOKS
Department BS 2-80
1230 Avenue of the Americas
New York, N.Y. 10020

Please send me the books I have checked above. I am enclosing
$_____(please add 50¢ to cover postage and handling for each order.
N.Y.S. and N.Y.C. residents please add appropriate sales tax). Send check
or money order—no cash or C.O.D.'s please. Allow up to six weeks for
delivery.

NAME_____

ADDRESS_____

CITY_____ STATE/ZIP_____

BS 2-80

The Site of the Biggest Mail Heist in History

POSTMARK: NEW YORK N.Y. 10022 — SEP 24 '79

Was it the Perfect Crime?

New York, N.Y. 10022—the richest postal district in the world and Jeff Grant masterminded an unbelievable heist: the hijack of every mail truck in the district on the first Monday of the month, the day the mail loads are heaviest. And it looked like Grant and his crack gang of white-collar crooks were going to slip away unnoticed with $20 million, until one of the hijacked trucks exploded at the final checkpoint!

What follows is a nerve-shattering race against time as the crooks hurry to cover their tracks and the cops turn up suspicious body after body.

You'll be trembling on the edge of your chair as the drama unfolds in NEW YORK, N.Y. 10022—the most ingenious, most exciting thriller of the decade.

NEW YORK, N.Y. 10022 by Steve Kahn   #82938/$2.50

POCKET BOOKS